D1547197

ACROSS
THE
COVERED
BRIDGE

A Novel in Nine Stories

FIRST EDITION

Copyright©2024 Sally Stiles
All rights reserved. This book, or parts thereof,
may not be reproduced without written permission.
Published in the USA by Pale Horse Books.

ISBN 978-1-939917-32-4

Other books by Sally Stiles
available through Pale Horse Books,
Barnes & Noble and Amazon.com.

Like a Mask Dancing — a Tanzanian Story
Plunge! – a memoir
The Haiku Guide to Williamsburg
The Haiku Guide to Cruising (The Pacific
Northwest)
Haiku Guide to the Inside Passage
Crazeman in the Bottle

Cover photograph by Louise Crowley
and formatted by the author
Author photo by Lisa W. Cumming.

ACROSS THE COVERED BRIDGE

Sally Stiles

Pale Horse Books

"The hardest thing to learn in life
is which bridge to cross
and which to burn."
—*Bertrand Russell*

This is a work of fiction. Names, characters, businesses, places, events, locales, and incidents are either the products of the author's imagination or used in a fictitious manner. Any resemblance to actual persons, living or dead, or actual events is purely coincidental.

The stories in this work are fictionally linked (both directly and indirectly) to a special New England town where I was privileged to live.

The characters are connected by their relationships, their aspirations and their need to understand and to be understood.

For
all the courageous artists
who challenged me
to look a little deeper

TABLE OF CONTENTS

WHAT SONIA TREASURES

I wasn't always Sonia Langhorne. In 1950, I was Sonia Salter, a Brooklyn-born, green-eyed, brown-haired, typical high school junior who was apparently descended on my father's side from an infamous British slave-trader and privateer.

Although I may have had an adventurous ancestry, my greatest aspiration that year was to avoid flunking Algebra II. I risked nothing more courageous than tapping an unexceptional boy on the shoulder to ask him to dance at a sock hop in the gym. But the late-May night when the DJ slipped Nat King Cole's new single, "Mona Lisa," into the mix, I became inspired. I was determined to learn the answer to the questions raised in that song. Was

Mona Lisa lonely? Was she hiding a broken heart? Did her dreams die on her doorstep? Or was she tempting a lover?

I knew almost nothing of DaVinci except that he lived a long time ago, painted religious pictures and wanted to fly like a bird, but that summer I went to the library and checked out a book with a picture of his *Mona Lisa*. Then, with my mother's Brownie Hawkeye camera, I photographed the painting from the book and taped the picture on my mirror until I could almost imitate her mystic smile. I thought it made me look intriguing, if not alluring enough to tempt a lover.

Only someone as young, as naive as I was, would try to replicate the most famous painting in the world, but I drew her face over and over again. Toward the end of the summer, I rummaged through the back of my mother's closet for unopened tubes of paint, unused brushes and watercolor paper my grandmother had given me years before. My first painting of the *Mona Lisa* looked like Raggedy Ann draped in a black hijab.

I signed up for an art class my senior year and was still trying to paint that face. I suppose my teacher became weary of those so-similar portraits, which is why she sent me back to the library to expand my repertoire. As a result, I tried to copy Claude Monet's clouds, then Vincent van Gogh's stars, Georgia O'Keeffe's poppies and, finally,

Georges Seurat's shimmering water. It didn't occur to me at the time that I could create my own clouds, stars, flowers and water.

Over Christmas break that year, I took the subway into Manhattan and went to the Metropolitan Museum. Back in 1929, Louisine Havemeyer had made a significant bequest to the Met—invaluable old masters and a multitude of works by French impressionists. One was Paul Cezanne's sweeping *Mont Sainte-Victoire and the Viaduct of the Arc River Valley* and another was his heavy, color-laden *Rocks at Fontainebleau*. When I stepped into the impressionist gallery and saw those two paintings, I fell in love with Paul Cezanne.

Cezanne invited me to wander through the French countryside, stroll a dirt path by a river, then climb a distant mountain. Halfway up that mountain, I rested on a boulder beneath sheltering trees.

When I came home, I started painting boulders as I imagined Cezanne might have painted them. I layered deep blues and purples and added daubs of green, dashes of orange. I was having fun—until I tried to imitate the trees that grew between the rocks. His slender pines seemed to dance to the wind. Mine brooded, sighed.

That year, my father, while working as a sous-chef at Lundy's, keeled over backwards. His apron was spotless, and his carving knife was still firmly wedged in the center of a lobster tail, but he perished on the kitchen floor. Since money was tight, I thought I should find a job. But, at Mother's insistence, I applied and was accepted as a Freshman at Pratt Institute in September, 1951. Pratt was my only option over other art schools because I could save money by living at home.

♦♦♦

In mid-November, at a required lecture on the metaphysics of art, I met Logan Langhorne, a senior philosophy major at NYU. He was working his way through school delivering for his father's Bronx business, Bright Day Laundry & Dry Cleaning.

With shoulder-length hair, a ragged mustache and large amber eyes, Logan looked like a forerunner of the Beatles' George Harrison. Being four years older than me, he seemed sophisticated. Smart. He also seemed sensitive, even gentle.

We took weekend walks around the city. We went to museums and occasionally to a movie. Our relationship remained platonic, which I chalked up to the fact that I was living at home in Brooklyn, and he was living at home in the Bronx. Since I'd never been comfortable with awkward groping in awkward places, I was fine with holding hands, occasional hugs and long goodnight kisses.

In May, we saw *The African Queen* at the Capitol Theater and, as we left the show, he put his arm around my shoulder and mimicked Humphrey Bogart: "Nothin' a man can't do if he sets his mind to it." I laughed, thinking that Logan was being flirtatious.

Afterwards, we had dinner at Katz's Delicatessen on Ludlow Street. It was us and sixty or so others squeezed into little tables beneath pictures of the rich and famous with members of the Katz family. Although Logan spent more time gazing at the photographs than at me, I was too smitten to recognize what his fascination with those pictures might portend.

◆◆◆

As soon as Logan graduated from NYU, he took off for India, Pakistan and Japan to delve into Eastern religions. He didn't ask me to wait for him to return, and I only received two postcards during the eleven months he was gone. One was of the Great Buddha at Kamakura and the other of belly dancers in Mumbai. Neither included words like "I love you" or "I miss you."

I plodded through my sophomore year without much success in learning all I wanted to know about painting. Neither did I come any closer to forgetting about Logan.

Then, on an unusually hot Friday in late May, I was up at the Guggenheim attempting to make sense of a Kandinsky for an assignment. I gave up an hour before my 3:00 class and took the Lexington Avenue IRT subway downtown, heading for Brooklyn. I was sitting in the side-facing seat next to the door, checking out the latest Miss Rheingold ad, her hair perfectly coiffed, her improbably white teeth smiling down at me. I was in no mood to return her smile.

When the train stopped at Grand Central, a skinny guy wearing tan shorts and a bright yellow Gaucho shirt stepped in. He carried a little white box. And, as he slid into the seat across from me, I realized it was Logan.

When he saw me, he jumped up and grasped the hanging strap in front of me while other passengers jostled him in their search for a seat. He leaned down toward me, his eyes sincere. "Sonia," he said, "I've been thinking about you all day. And here you are. Serendipity. I believe in serendipity, don't you?"

The grizzled man on the seat beside me shook his head and muttered a garlicky "Hmmph!" I inched as far away from him as I could.

"I assumed you were still trekking around Asia," I said to Logan.

"I wore out my sneakers and couldn't afford another pair."

I looked at his feet. He was wearing black plastic sandals.

When we neared Union Square, Logan grabbed my hand. "Let's get off here."

"I can't. I have a class in Brooklyn at 3:00."

"Sonia, I have in this box a delicacy we should share," Logan said, a smile spreading across his face and lighting up his amber eyes.

The garlicky old guy next to me jabbed me with his elbow. I jumped up.

I skipped class. We walked to Washington Square and settled on a bench far from the arch where a doomsday fanatic was haranguing passersby. Logan unwrapped the string on the little white box. Inside was a matcha green tea cake. He produced two plastic forks from his pocket.

"Do you always carry around two forks?" I asked.

He smiled again. "I told you I believe in serendipity."

After we'd devoured the cake, I asked him what he learned in his travels.

He unfolded the little box, tore it into strips and quickly refolded it into a series of origami squares. Then he pulled a Swiss Army knife from his pocket, punched a hole in each end of the cardboard and tied the ends together with the string from the box. He slipped the bracelet around my wrist. I spun it around and around, delighted with its asymmetry.

Finally, he spoke. "In my travels, I learned that I don't want to be poor." He swallowed, looked away, then looked at me again with such intensity I thought he might be going into a trance. "I learned that I missed you, Sonia."

"You spent a year studying Eastern religions in interesting places and sent me only two postcards, yet you say you missed me."

He nodded. "It's true. I missed you. A lot."

I responded with my best Mona Lisa smile, then asked him how long he'd been back.

"About a week," he said.

"You've been back a week, but I didn't hear from you, so you must not have missed me all that much. And if you hadn't run into me on the subway—"

"Sonia, the other thing I learned is that, as soon as I find a job, I want to marry you."

"Oh, Logan, you can't be serious."

"Nothin' a man can't do if he sets his mind to it," he said. Then he kissed me, a kiss that tingled every nerve in my body—and I was thinking that in his travels he must have learned some things he wasn't mentioning.

Two days later he called and told me he was made vice-president of Bright Day Laundry and Dry Cleaning, and three months later we gathered with his parents and my mother in Central Park to be married by a Daoshi, a Taoist priest. The service lasted ten minutes, and afterwards the Daoshi led us to the carousel. Logan hopped on a black horse and caught the brass ring. For the first time all day, my mother beamed.

♦♦♦

As a new bride married to an interesting man, I was happy our first two years. We rented a walkup studio apartment in SoHo. Logan commuted to his father's store in the Bronx. I snagged a job at a gallery on 10th Street and began to learn a good deal more about art than I'd learned in school. While occasionally I still dreamed of becoming a painter, I began to believe that my talent might lie in championing artists who were more innovative, more daring, than I.

I was noticeably pregnant by mid-summer of 1955, five months before our child was expected. The gallery manager didn't fire me but kept looking at my stomach and asking me how long I expected to stay. He was clearly relieved when I resigned in August.

Then, in October, two months before Will was born, Logan began to acquire new friends— influential friends—including an up-and-coming investment banker, a commercial real-estate agent on the rise, a senior vice-president of the hottest ad agency in town. He was invited to the 21 Club for lunch, to Delmonico's for dinner.

Logan clearly meant what he'd said that day on the bench in Washington Square. He didn't like being poor. He shaved his mustache and cut his hair short, bought two new suits at Saks, a handful of ties at Bonwit Teller, a raincoat at Burberry. He wasn't George Harrison anymore.

♦♦♦

By the time Will turned two, Logan had amassed enough money to buy—with a hefty mortgage—a home in Murray Hill. Shortly thereafter, he enrolled us as members of St. Thomas Episcopal church. On Easter eve the next year we renewed our vows at St. Thomas.

"I feel better now," Logan said, "knowing that the Christian God has joined us together and no man can put us asunder."

I laughed. "Did you have a particular man in mind, Logan?" I had a husband and a young son to care for and wasn't looking for a man to persuade me to leave Logan. But I began to become acquainted with a whole cadre of men who were enticing Logan down a path I was dubious of following.

His first goal was to expand his father's business into each of the five boroughs—from the Bronx to Manhattan, then Brooklyn and Queens. He reached Staten Island on our tenth anniversary, and, that year, his parents moved from their apartment in Yonkers to a big house in the Bronx. Logan suggested that my mother could move to the city and become assistant-manager of the Manhattan store, but she was enamored with a bartender at a restaurant she now managed in Brooklyn. They moved, rent-free, into the apartment above the Brooklyn dry cleaning store.

♦♦♦

On our fifteenth anniversary in 1968, after dinner at La Grenouille, Ramon, our newly acquired chauffeur, turned left on Park Avenue, heading up town. "Where is he going?" I asked Logan. "The au pair is expecting us home by ten."

"I have something to show you," Logan said.

Ramon turned left again on 72nd[th] Street, headed down Fifth for several blocks, then turned left again on a side street. He stopped outside a building just off Fifth Avenue which appeared to be comprised of rows of square glass boxes divided by thin strips of steel. Cranes hovered over the older stone buildings on either side where the top floors were being demolished.

Logan motioned me out of the car, told Ramon that we wouldn't be gone long, then took my hand and led me up the steps to the glass building. A tall, steely-eyed doorman in a blue uniform greeted him by name and opened the door. Inside, past a bank of brass mailboxes, there was a step down into a sunken sitting area where two white leather couches faced each other with a glass and brass coffee table between them. Beyond, above the two brass-door elevators, a long rectangular painting of off-white waves splashed across an off-white painted canvas.

"What are we doing here, Logan?" I had a feeling I wouldn't like his answer.

But he didn't answer. Instead, he pulled me into the elevator and pushed the button for the 14th floor. When the door closed, he leaned down and kissed me, then slipped a brass key into my hand. "Happy Anniversary," he said.

The elevator whooshed us smoothly up through the floors. When it stopped, Logan led me down the hall to #1402, the second of only two units on the floor. He took a key from his pocket and turned it in the deadbolt lock. Then he told me to put my key in the lower lock. The door opened onto a foyer with a white marble floor and matching walls. On the right wall there was a large empty niche which, I assumed, was meant to house a rare marble sculpture.

Beyond the foyer, a large, white-carpeted room was furnished with white leather couches and chairs and glass side tables. On a glass and brass coffee table facing a glassed-in fireplace, there was a free-form Baccarat crystal vase overflowing with red roses. I suspected the same decorator who furnished the lobby had furnished this condominium—and probably provided the roses as well. But at least there was no minimalist abstract painting of off-white waves over the fireplace.

Logan stopped and looked into the empty sunken room next to the kitchen. "I thought you'd like to keep your grandmother's Shaker dining table," he said, "so I didn't buy anything new for the dining room there. I also left the second guest room empty for your grandmother's sleigh bed."

"Logan, you bought this place. And you bought all this furniture without letting me know?"

He nodded and grinned. "I wanted to surprise you."

"Why, Logan, why?"

"We deserve it," he said and smiled again.

"But what about our brownstone in Murray Hill?"

"I'm turning it into four apartments," he said. "I already have the permit."

"But, Logan—"

"It's a great investment," he said.

He walked over to the large square window overlooking the city. "Isn't this spectacular? Look, you can see the corner of the Plaza Hotel—and the zoo is just through those trees over there. Sonia, from here you can walk to the Museum of Modern Art, to the Met. You're going to love this place."

He opened the door to the balcony. I couldn't hear him over the sound of revving cars and honking horns. When he stepped back inside and closed the door, he grinned again and said, "I've already ordered the hot tub."

Logan obviously didn't know how much I would miss our relatively quiet side street in Murray Hill—the old, narrow buildings with entrances graced by distinctive stonework, stylish doors, bright awnings or elegant porticos, and the linden trees along the sidewalk—their fragile white flowers appearing in late June. Our son, Will, had friends from the adjoining buildings, and, after school, they played together at the combination basketball/tennis courts just around the corner.

"When do we have to move?"

"I figured it would take you a couple of months to get this place settled and looking like home, so the contractor is holding off on the Murray Hill place until November."

I felt as if I were being moved to a different city with different people, different lifestyles, different values. There was no way I could make this place the home we'd had in Murray Hill. I loved our old brownstone despite its uneven floors, small closets, stairs to climb to the kitchen, more stairs to the bedrooms. Logan, though, was obviously thrilled with this upscale condominium. And, as much as I cringed at his decision, I knew that, to please him, I would eventually figure out how to make it into a place where we could live.

Logan insisted that I hire Truman Capote's decorator to finish furnishing the condo. She wanted me to purchase an alabaster Greek goddess for the marble alcove niche. Instead, I found a large, polished wood sculpture of Hotei, Japanese god of Good Fortune, with his significant belly and linen sack of treasures. Not only did Logan let the

Japanese god stay, but I often saw him stop at the entryway to rub Hotei's belly.

◆◆◆

Soon after we moved in, Logan changed our church membership from St. Thomas to the Episcopal Cathedral of St. John the Devine, further uptown. When his father died later that year, Logan sold the dry-cleaning business and invested the profits and his inheritance in ever-bigger real-estate deals in the city. He bought a building near Katz's Deli, and a picture of him with Lennie Katz and Mayor Ed Koch appeared on the restaurant wall.

By age forty-five, Logan was no longer skinny, and I hadn't worked at a gallery—or anywhere else—in years.

So, why did I follow my husband on this journey into a life which grew more alien year by year? A good deal of the time, the Logan who'd pulled me off that subway car continued to enchant me. He still had sincere amber eyes, a ready smile, and he'd never lost his talent for kissing. Also, in front of two priests representing two separate religions I'd made a promise to love him for richer or poorer. I don't like to break promises.

As hard as it is to admit it now, Logan's newly acquired status began to feed my ego. I started to cull designer fashions from the best houses and pulled strings to see—and be seen—at the latest shows on opening night. I even scanned the society columns for my picture and liked feeling significant when it appeared.

I enjoyed being welcomed by name when I entered Tiffany's, Four Seasons or Twenty-One. Oddly enough, I was just as pleased that the security guard in the French Impressionist gallery at the Met knew me by name. At least once a month I'd visit the Guggenheim, the Museum of Modern Art, or, most often, the Metropolitan, where Paul Cezanne's landscapes still inspired me. I even began to imagine myself painting alongside Cezanne at the edge of his river, gazing through slender pine trees at his mountain beyond.

Logan bought his mother a home in Bonita Springs on the gulf coast of Florida and took ownership of her big house in Riverdale. Beginning the next September, Will and I spent most of our time at the Bronx house so he could attend Riverdale Country school.

The next year, though Logan had enrolled Will in a boarding school in Connecticut, I still spent more time in Riverdale than in the condo in the city. I decorated the home with paintings by the artists I'd worked with at the gallery and bought some drawing pencils and a sketchbook. When alone in Riverdale, I filled pages with Cezanne's mountain and became much better at drawing his trees.

◆◆◆

In 1993, three months before our 40th anniversary, Logan's secretary called me. "Would you rather stay at the George V or the Ritz?"

"Is this a quiz?"

"Mr. Langhorne asked me to check with you. He wants your trip to France to be special."

Either the trip to France was meant to be an anniversary surprise, or he'd forgotten to mention it to me. I never had a chance to ask. That night, I was at the house in Riverdale, and Logan stayed in the city. I had a Light Opera Society board meeting the next morning, so Ramon picked me up in the limo at eight o'clock. Since I was early, I told him to drop me off at the condo. I wandered through the rooms, looking for Logan. Since he never left for work until ten o'clock, I was surprised he wasn't there. The first thing that popped into my head was that he'd spent the night at someone else's condo, exercising his talent for kissing.

I stepped out onto our balcony to look over the city and ponder his absence. There he was, face down, naked in the hot tub. A half-eaten dish of funazushi sat on the rim of the tub, and a single pair of mother of pearl chopsticks floated above the drain. The autopsy revealed a ruptured cerebral aneurysm. Logan was only sixty-four.

I was on my own for the first time in forty years—on my own to make decisions I'd allowed Logan to make for me. I longed to see his amber eyes, his assured smile again. I yearned for his kisses, his decisions. As social invitations diminished, I also began to realize the difference in status accorded the wife of Logan Langhorne and his widow. I began to consider alternate paths to travel—but each time I was stopped mid-way by an overwhelming desire to make amends to my son.

When Logan had sent Will off to a prestigious boarding school, I didn't oppose his decision, even though I felt we'd abandoned our only child. Later, when Will chose teaching at Emory University over working for his father, Logan was incensed. He argued with Will, telling him he was losing out on a great opportunity to build a fortune, to create an exceptional life. When Will wasn't swayed, I felt that Logan began to grow indifferent to his son— and that was harder for me to bear than their arguments. Our visits with Will, his wife, Elaine, and our grandson Charlie became less frequent and more strained. At Logan's funeral, Will seemed detached from his emotions, as if his father had died long ago. I was at a loss as to how to comfort him.

◆◆◆

In early December, I called Will to ask him if I might visit him soon to search out houses in his neighborhood. "Elaine and I would welcome you in Atlanta, Mother," he said, "and there are probably some suitable properties for sale. But let me think this through a bit."

He called me back half an hour later. "Mother, about you coming here to live. I believe that if you move now, you'd trade being Mrs. Logan Langhorne for being Will Langhorne's mother and Charlie Langhorne's grandmother. I think you'd do rather well as Sonia Langhorne." He paused, as if to let what he said sink in. "Do you understand what I'm saying?"

"I think I do, Will. I'd be interfering with your life."

"No, Mom. That's not what I meant. I can help you find a place now, but you have the means to do what you want and, for the first time in years, nobody is holding you back. I want to see you happy in your own right. When you need us, we'll be here for you."

His faith in me gave me the courage to believe that a new Sonia Langhorne deserved a try. While I didn't trust her yet—after all, I hardly knew her—I would begin to look for her at sea.

I sailed to Southampton on the Cunard Line, uninspired by the tedious days crossing the ocean and uncomfortably alone in the large seventh-deck suite Logan's former secretary booked for me. I took the short Air France flight from London to Paris where I stayed at a reasonably priced Novotel near the Louvre, exploring every corner of the museum, always circling back to return Mona Lisa's smile. I became intrigued with the rest of the painting—her eyes, her veil, and, especially, the landscape behind her. Did the road on her right connect to the bridge on her left? Why were the trees and water on her left higher than those on her right? What was behind her that nobody could see?

Four days later I rented a Renault and headed south. I walked through Avignon and Aix en Provence, following Cezanne's footsteps. I gazed at Mont Sainte Victoire across the Arc River valley. Then I journeyed toward the coast.

In Marseilles, on a whim, I traded most of my inheritance—the limo, the condo, some rare Persian rugs, a fistful of stocks and a safe deposit box full of jewelry—for a painting of a mountain, a valley and a tree. It was a splendid trade.

The following spring, eight months after Logan died, I prepared to move to a small cottage in New Hampshire, along with my newly purchased masterpiece, my grandmother's Shaker dining set and her sleigh bed, Logan's mother's Tanzanite ring and the frayed and yellowing origami bracelet Logan had placed on my wrist all those years ago.

I have no idea if I made the right decision, but I expect that every night I'll smile at that painting before going to bed, wondering at my good fortune to look at it whenever I please. Then, before I turn out the light, I'll open the top drawer of my nightstand, pull out the cardboard bracelet Logan

made all those years ago, gently press it to my lips
and wonder what might have been.

Sally Stiles

WHAT SONIA ENVISIONS

The movers are due in the morning, and my refrigerator is empty, so I accept an invitation for dinner at Trevor and Meredith Reston's house. While I find their parties tiresome and would rather stay home, even skip dinner, I hope to have a chance to talk to Meredith's brother, Conrad.

My late husband, Logan, avoided the Restons completely. "They're not my people," he said. After attending a few of their gatherings, I realized that Trevor and Meredith and their assortment of country club comrades weren't my people, either. But I always looked forward to seeing Conrad, a shy, retired professor of Classical Studies at Columbia University.

Over the years, Conrad helped relieve the tedium of party prattle when we had an opportunity to chat for a little while. He'd talk to me about the arts, about literature and philosophy. He found contentment in living an unpretentious life—the kind of contentment he inspired me to seek by my impending move from the city to a modest cottage in New Hampshire.

The cottage is surrounded by forests of tall white pines and clumps of paper birch. Morning mist rises off the river, and beyond, pastel clouds cast shadows across the mountains of Vermont. The population is about 950 people—farmers, craftsmen, scholars, artists. My nearest neighbors will be beaver, deer and horned owls. I think Conrad would like it there. I'm hoping he'll come up for a visit.

But when I walk into the Reston's drawing room, I see Conrad lying on the divan next to the fireplace. He's wrapped in a Mackenzie tartan blanket, and his head lies to one side like a stunned bird. The open book beneath his right hand is turned upside down. His gold-rimmed glasses have slipped from the bridge of his thin, scholarly nose, and his eyes are closed. His mouth set in contemplation— for eternity, I fear.

I stand at the door watching for some sign of air coming from Conrad's mouth or nose, some indication that his chest is moving. Nothing. And nobody seems to notice. Nobody notices me, either, until Meredith Reston finally shifts in her oversized Hepplewhite armchair at the foot of the divan. She places her martini on the Florentine table beside her, runs a hand studded with diamonds through her glossy silver hair, then finally looks up toward the door and calls out, "Come in, Sonia, come in!" Her voice sparkles like ice in a crystal goblet.

There's a slight movement from the divan. Has Conrad moved his head? Or has Meredith jiggled him ever so slightly?

I remain at the door and peer closely at Meredith, trying to discover some sign of distress over her brother's condition. But she's wearing her Perle Mesta look, her blue eyes flashing the promise of a brilliant evening.

"Come in, darling!" she says. "Everyone, Sonia's just returned from a fabulous—just fabulous!—trip abroad. We can't wait to hear all about it!" Her other guests, Blanche and Harold Underthorpe, Patsy and Phil Maurier, glance up briefly. Blanche frowns. Patsy smiles. They continue their conversation. Harold and Phil raise their tumblers to their mouths. Conrad doesn't move.

It's too bizarre to believe that Conrad has been left to stiffen as the party gets underway. I walk toward him. Patsy rises and shakes her head of orange curls while gesticulating with both hands. I duck and back away. "That rude upstart they hired for the locker room at the club. I've drafted a petition." She snorts and turns to Blanche, her voice insistent. "I'm sure you'll sign."

Blanche reaches out for Patsy's fluttering hand. "Of course, dear. Now, sit back down and tell me how the preparations are coming along for the Memorial Day ball."

I walk over to the end of the divan and lean down to get a better look at Conrad. His cheekbones appear as fragile as the flower of a paperwhite, his skin as transparent.

"Meredith. Your brother—have you called the emergency squad?" She either doesn't hear me or chooses not to. She's sipping a martini and staring at her grandfather's portrait over the mantel. He was an Anglican bishop with soft hands and dull, gray eyes.

"Meredith!"

She turns to me, startled. Again, there's a faint movement of Conrad's head. "Sonia, dear, how fabulous you look—but you always do. I'll bet you bought that darling dress in Paris. What do you call that green?"

I look down at my dress, the matching shoes and duster. "Turquoise," I say. Just like the veins in poor Conrad's hands.

"Meredith," I plead. "How long has Conrad—"

She interrupts me. "Vodka and Water?"

Before I have a chance to answer, Meredith turns her head and shouts toward the dining room. "Trevor! Sonia's here. Could you be a dear and bring her a vodka and water?"

"Vodka and water!" she repeats, her voice loud enough to wake King Tut. Patsy, Blanche, Phil and Harold raise their heads. Conrad doesn't stir.

Meredith directs me to the matching Hepplewhite chair beside her. "Your brother," I say. "I think he's slipped into a coma. Or worse."

She pats my hand. "He's just resting up for dinner. A little nap."

Before I can suggest otherwise, Trevor Reston is standing in front of me, holding a drink. "Vodka and water, right?" he says. He's wearing his company manners along with a maroon cashmere vee-neck sweater, white summer slacks and a navy blazer. He bends over to kiss my cheek—a stretch for his six-feet four. I grab the drink; he misses my cheek. I take a gulp of the vodka. It's straight gin. I put the drink down on the Florentine table.

"Trevor," I whisper. He leans down again. "I'm worried about Conrad."

"Conrad?" he replied. "Yes, he's getting on a bit, but doing fine. Just fine."

◆◆◆

Though Conrad and Meredith are co-owners of the house they inherited from their parents, Conrad's bedroom and book-lined study are up the back stairs behind the kitchen—small rooms which were former servants' quarters. During cocktail hour, Conrad tended to disappear.

After a discreet interval, I'd slip out, climb the stairs and knock on his study door. He'd invite me in and ask me some question I had no idea how to answer. Once he asked if I thought any worthwhile ideas had been advanced since Plautus died in 184 B.C. Another time he asked if I knew of an accurate translation of *Antigone*.

Most of the time, however, he'd motion me to sit in the chair by his desk, then pick up an open book and begin to read out loud. I'd interrupt with questions which he'd patiently answer.

The last time I entered his study, Conrad was reading *For Whom the Bell Tolls*. The book was open at the end of Chapter twenty-seven, where Lieutenant Berrendo ordered the dead soldiers to be decapitated and their bodies packed out on the horses.

Conrad read: "(Berrendo) made the sign of the cross again and as he walked down the hill he said five Our Fathers and five Hail Marys for the repose of the soul of his dead comrade. He did not wish to stay to see his orders being carried out."

I've tried to read *For Whom the Bell Tolls* several times but couldn't suffer through the chilling descriptions of the Spanish Civil War. I asked Conrad if he didn't think it was painful for Hemingway to write this book. Before he had chance to answer, I also asked him if he ever wondered how Picasso could stand before his *Guernica* for two months, painting the anguished figures which depicted the brutality of this same war.

Without hesitating, Conrad calmly answered both of my questions. "Aristotle said, 'to be angry with the right person, and to the right degree, and at the right time for the right purpose is not within everybody's power and is not easy.' Picasso and Hemingway were righteously enraged, and I believe they held nothing back to create a broader community of rage."

Before I had a chance to think thorough what he said, I asked him another question. 'Do you think Jackson Pollock was enraged when he painted *War?*"

Conrad sighed and closed his book "All of Pollock's paintings make me think of a tortured man on a binge. With *War* he simulated Guernica figures, added a pyre of human bodies and scrawled images in red, yellow and black all over the canvas. I believe he was trying to one-up Picasso."

Conrad looked over at a painting on his wall—a painting I had given him. It was a gentle abstract of a forest glen. Then he looked back at me and shook his head. "Sadly, Pollock was a man of great potential but little restraint—nourished, no doubt, by alcohol. Large quantities of alcohol." Conrad stood. "That reminds me that we should probably return downstairs to the party."

When we entered the parlor, the conversation ceased for a moment while the other guests looked at us closely. Meredith rose from her chair. She approached us and spoke in a stage whisper, asking the question she always asked when we'd escaped a gathering. "What have you two been doing?"

"Reading, of course," Conrad answered as he always did. He shrugged his shoulders, as if it were perfectly normal to leave a party to go upstairs to read.

◆◆◆

Tonight, as the guests head for the dining room, I approach the divan. I stand over Conrad and recite a line from Marcus Annaeus Lucanus, a line that, on occasion, Conrad had recited to me.

The gods conceal from man
the happiness of death
that they may endure life.

When Conrad doesn't stir on hearing these words, I'm more convinced than ever that he isn't just resting. I slip into the adjoining library, pick up the phone and dial 911 to report an emergency at the Reston home. I return to the divan, close the book beside his right hand—a classic edition of *The Divine Comedy*—then fold his glasses and place them on top of the book.

"I'll miss you so much, my friend," I say. I brush my fingers over his cheek then head for the front door. I glance back at the dining room. There are two empty chairs. Clearly one chair is for me and one for Conrad. Nobody seems concerned that both are vacant until Meredith turns in her seat at the head of the table. "Sonia, dear, why are you leaving before dinner?"

"Because Conrad—." Before I have a chance to finish, Patsy Maurier calls out, "Don't forget that the Memorial Day Ball committee meets on Monday at noon in the Dahlia Room. We need your artistic contributions."

"The moving van is coming tomorrow," I mutter. "I'm sure you'll do fine without me."

I look back at Conrad once more, knowing that he'll never read to me again. I can only hope he'll matriculate into some great university in the sky where he'll find his way into a dining club with Plutarch, Dante and Sophocles.

I run down the front steps, hail a cab and, once home, call the Reston residence. But the phone is busy or, more likely, off the hook. I try to sleep, but toss all night, tangled in the single sheet I've left on the bed for my last night in the city.

In the morning, I try to call the Restons again, but still there's no answer. The movers unplug my phone, and I take off for my little cottage in New Hampshire.

Two days later, after the movers pull out of my driveway, I head down to the general store and pick up a copy of the *New York Times*. My dear Conrad—his whole life—has been reduced to a 12-line obituary. He deserves so much more. His parents are named, his sister, his profession, his book on Plutarch as a priest. What's left out is his influence on generations of students—and how much he meant to me.

I've moved to New Hampshire to find a place to slow down. To think. To live more authentically. I can only imagine what it would have been like had Conrad followed me here. Perhaps we would have explored the shelves of the Dartmouth College library, taken long walks, skied cross-country in the wintertime. Maybe we would have paddled the river in a lightweight canoe, stopped for a picnic lunch on shore.

I sometimes envision evenings sitting side by side in Adirondack chairs, sipping red wine and watching the sun set over Mount Ascutney. Sometimes I sense Logan in the chair beside me; other times, it's Conrad, reading aloud and asking me questions I wish I knew how to answer.

I make up our conversations. Tonight, Conrad and I talk about how we will spend our remaining years. We agree that we'll never attend another of Meredith Reston's dinner parties. We both laugh at the very idea.

Sally Stiles

WHAT CLARE SEES

Since he started his new business, Riley to the Rescue, my husband heads to the fancy old estates in the Colony most every day. Some houses there are pretty near 300 years old and sure need a lot of rescuing. Other days he goes down to the Flat where the log cabins and weatherboard bungalows barely hang on from one mud season to the next.

Every morning after breakfast, in rain, snow, sunshine or mud, Riley takes off in his old blue Ford Ranger, the truck bed loaded down with toolboxes full of paint brushes and sanders and putty knives and wrenches and such. He toots the horn and waves at me from the edge of the gravel. When he gets home, he pops open a can of Hamm's and sits by the fire. When the weather allows, we sit outside on the porch swing, and he tells me what he's seen and heard.

Mondays and Thursdays, I drive across the old covered bridge to work at the library in Vermont where I sort out the books and put them back on the shelves. I've got a knack for remembering numbers. I was just a volunteer at first, but the head librarian said she liked the care I took putting the books in their right places. "Clare," she said, "would you consider working for us a couple of days a week? We can offer you $3.50 an hour." I said sure.

The library is a hushed-up place. If anyone even looks like they're talking, we give 'em a wicked stare, so most of what I know about the goings on in this corner of New Hampshire, I learn from Riley.

Riley's friendly with most everyone, even if he's just met them. I'm one for holding off being too cozy with folks 'til I get to know who they really are.

My dad—he's gone now seven years—raised hogs and chickens, ran the snowplow, up before dawn winter mornings. With his balding head, stubbly chin, most teeth missing, he wasn't much to look at, but he sure worked hard, though his work paid little, and we had our fill of being snubbed. Most folks around here are nice enough, but there's the ritzy that look down on regular folk like Riley and me, and the ritzy who are welcoming so long as we don't step too far into their parlors. Then there's the poor folk that act like they're ritzy. I know from experience that it takes some time to figure out who you can count as a real friend.

♦♦♦

It's a Tuesday morning in June when Mrs. Langhorne comes bouncing up the gravel to our place in a twenty-year-old red 1974 Volvo Estate that used to belong to Doc Weston, the horse vet. Riley says Doc put a hundred fifty thousand miles on that car before he sold it. "It'll go another hundred thousand," Riley says. I believe it. Riley knows a good bit about cars.

Even though she's driving that rattly old wagon, when she gets out of the car, I figure Mrs. Langhorne for having money. I take one look at her big brown handbag, soft as the ear of a new-born Holstein. Didn't come from K-Mart or J.C. Penney's. And those shiny, pointed high-heeled shoes? Not fake leather.

The closer she comes, the more I realize she's sort of jerry-rigged: short, with a long neck, flat chin and skinny legs. Her hair is curled up tight as a rag rug against her head, a few strands of gray woven into the brown. She's wearing sunglasses the likes of which I've never seen—blue-tinted mirrors in wire granny frames—and when she whips 'em off, I see her eyes are green with little touches of brown, like the skins of avocados stacked up in a bin at the Price Chopper.

She says she's wanting Riley because her sink is leaking. Her words whoosh out like a train rushing by. "I tried to fix that old sink," she says, "but, try as I might, I couldn't wrench off the rusty pipe." I'm twice Mrs. Langhorne's size, a good bit younger, probably three times stronger, but I can't imagine trying to wrench a pipe off a sink. That's a job for Riley. He knows just about all there is to know about pipes and sinks and such.

Mrs. Langhorne tells me she's come up from New York and bought the old Trombley place. For the life of me, I can't recall the name Trombley. I'm trying to think which big old house has been for sale of late. A woman from New York with a purse and shoes like hers would have latched onto a fancy place once owned by one of the famous artists or writers or society folks that formed the Colony back in the 'twenties—back when they called our village "Little New York."

Mrs. Langhorne's voice rises like I'm hard of hearing. "I bought that sweet cottage up the hill from the cemetery."

It dawns on me that Mrs. Langhorne bought the little run-down house hidden in the woods halfway up the hill. You can just glimpse the red cedar shake siding and the pitched roof as you drive by. There's a lot of lichen growing on that roof. I'm puzzled now for sure as to why she'd buy such a tatty place.

I sneak a close look at her hands. Hands can tell a lot about folks. Mine are broad and freckled, comes with my ginger hair. Hers are smooth and thin, the nails polished ruby red. There's one good-sized blue stone set in gold on the fourth finger of her right hand, but no diamonds around it. And though I expect a whopper diamond on her left hand, all those fingers are bare. Maybe she's not so ritzy after all.

She catches me peering at her fingers and crosses her arms over her chest, hides her hands and says the strangest thing. "You pay for diamonds with your freedom, you know."

I wouldn't know, but I nod as if I agree.

Wednesday night, Riley comes home and grabs a Hamm's from the fridge. I join him out on the porch swing. Our place, up near the Hollow, gives us a nice view of the Connecticut River and Mount Ascutney over in Vermont, but only in wintertime after the leaves have turned and fallen from the sugar maples. Riley is looking hard at the trees.

"What do you see, Riley?" I ask.

"I see fresh syrup on my pancakes come spring," he says.

All I see is Riley, looking at bright green leaves.

He's wearing a pair of dungarees and his old blue sweatshirt, the one that says *Live Free or Die.* I don't care what Riley wears. Even drinking a Hamm's or two most nights, his belly is flat and his muscles hard. Peer at him sideways, and he looks just like the Indian on the old penny. His hair is thick and gold brown—like wheat ready to harvest. Lately I notice little touches of silver around his ears, making him look even more handsome.

I began to love Riley's gold-brown hair when we were in the same class in fourth grade. By 10th grade I was so fiercely in love I told everyone— except Riley—that we were going to be married. When he invited me to the Senior Prom, I thought I was headed for wedded bliss, but then Riley upped and joined the Navy without even telling me. I didn't hear from him until he flew back from San Diego after his two-year stint. In his pocket was a gold wedding band. Exactly my size.

Riley tells me he tended to Mrs. Langhorne's sink. "Took me darn near twenty minutes with a blow torch to wrench off that rusted pipe," he says, then swallows a big mouthful of beer. "That's a spunky lady," he says, then grins like he's teasing me. "She's even kind of handsome in an older womanly way."

"Hmmn," I say. "Maybe you oughta go see the eye doctor."

He just laughs and wipes his mouth with the back of his hand. "That lady's cabin needs a fair bit of work," he says. "It's right sparsely furnished, except for a skinny dining room table she tells me was made by Shakers in Watervliet, New York in 1796. She says it's special since it was her grandma's table. She's also got a big old bed that looks like a sleigh."

I tell Riley not to get too close to that bed. He laughs again. "Oh, Clare, our bed is bed enough for me." I give him a peck on the cheek and tell him I love him. What I don't tell him is that I'm planning to take a pie down to Mrs. Langhorne in the morning. I hope to get a closer look at her—and that bed.

I get up early the next morning, make Riley breakfast, wave him good-bye, pick the first of the crooknecks from the garden and set to making two sweet squash pies. I wrap one up in a red checkered napkin and set it on the passenger seat of my blue Subaru. Just as I round the bend by the beaver dam on Platt Road, I see Riley's truck pulling out of Mrs. Langhorne's driveway. I slow down and wait for him to reach the bottom of the hill before I coast down to her place.

I pull in slowly and look around. There's a stand of birch trees to the left of the house, then an open space where I glimpse a slice of the river and Mount Ascutney beyond. I circle a 60-foot cone-shaped white pine, thick of trunk and heavy with branches, then park by the front door. Beside the garage is the scruffy rectangle of a long-overgrown vegetable garden. If it's ever going to grow squash and carrots and cauliflower again, it's going to need some tilling, so I reckon Mrs. Langhorne will be calling Riley to the rescue. He grew up on a little corn and wheat farm in the Flat and knows all about tilling.

It takes three rings before Mrs. Langhorne opens the door. I hand over the pie. "Thank you so much," she says. "I haven't had pie in the longest time." She looks beyond me, out to the road as if expecting more folks, then says, "Can you come in, Clare? I'll make us some tea. Do you like oolong?"

"Sure," I say. "Whatever you're having." But I'm thinking ooo-who? Doesn't sound like real tea.

While she's heating the water on her old wood stove, I peek into the sitting room. There's a stiff-looking robin's egg blue couch in front of the fireplace, a couple of matching chairs. By the front window there's a tall, fancy wooden easel with flowers—pansies, from the look of them—whittled into the two front legs. The top is carved to look like a French lily—like you see on the license plates of folks coming down from Quebec. There's no picture sitting on that easel. I wonder why.

I step into the room far enough to peek around the corner for a quick look at the bed. It has a curved headboard and footboard, thick slabs of wood,

Birdseye maple from the look of it, and all four posts are carved into waves and curlicues and such. It looks comfy enough, but it's so tall I shudder thinking about turning over in my sleep and landing on the floor.

She comes out from the kitchen with a tray of tea served in dainty, gold-rimmed cups, and tiny slices of pie on tiny plates matching the cups. I sit down at the table, which is just a thin board on skinny legs, and the high-back chairs are none too steady. She hands me a white cloth napkin and a cup of tea, which is light green and smells like grass. I wonder if it's been steeped enough. I take a sip. It tastes like grass. To kill the taste, I take a bite of the pie, which is sweet enough, and the crust firm, but the filling is pale compared to my Hubbard. I tell Mrs. Langhorne I'll bring her a Hubbard pie as soon as the squash ripens.

I tell her gardening is tricky here in New Hampshire. "You don't dare put in your vegetables 'til after Memorial Day, and I've known frost to nip 'em the first week in September."

"Is that so?" she says. "I have a lot to learn about gardening."

I'm not surprised. Riley's taken me down to New York City a couple of times, and all I saw in the way of gardens were little pots of wilted flowers sitting on tiny balconies. I wondered what folks do all summer with no garden to tend.

Then it dawns on me that she has that swanky easel, and I know folks from New York can be artsy. "Are you a painter?" I ask.

"Maybe," she says. I mull that over, not sure if it means she won't tell me or she's wanting to learn how to paint.

"You've come to a place that fancies art," I say. "Augustus Saint-Gaudens, that famous sculptor, lived right up the hill over yonder."

"She looks out the window, toward the hill, then turns to me and changes the subject. "You must call me Sonia," she says. "We're near neighbors now."

I don't feel that's proper, her being one of Riley's customers. I don't call any of them by their first names. But I say my name is Clare.

"I know that, Clare," she says. She smiles—a small but kindlier smile than I expect.

Then she looks at me sideways, as if trying to decide to tell me more. I guess I pass whatever test she's giving me, because then she looks straight at me, her eyes steady. She starts right in. "I settled on buying this place because of a painting, a painting of a mountain rising up across a river valley. Logan, my husband, died suddenly—an aneurism. He'd planned a trip to France, and I decided to go anyway. I was walking around Marseille and saw a sign for an auction. I looked at the work going up for sale, and when I saw that painting, I knew I had to have it."

Again, she looks out the window, nods slightly, then takes a tiny bite from the end of the pie. "Oh," she says, "this is good country pie." I'm not sure exactly what she means, pie being pie, but I say it was Riley's mother's recipe. "Riley's mother never failed to make a good pie," I tell her, but I don't want to talk about pie. "You were telling me about a painting," I say.

She takes another bite, a bigger one this time, then looks straight at me again. "Well, I gave them a down payment and, when I got home, I sold some stuff, and when the painting arrived, I knew I had done the right thing."

She puts her fork into the rest of the pie on her plate and stuffs it in her mouth. Her chin moves up and down.

◆◆◆

Pictures are okay, but I prefer what I see in real life. We have a couple of pictures in the house. One Riley bought special for me was painted by that handsome Maxfield Parrish who lived just up the road. Died in '66. Well, it's not a picture Mr. Parrish actually painted, but a nice copy. There's a mountain and mill and a brook. It could be the old Blow Me Down gristmill on Route 12-A, next to the cemetery down from Mrs. Langhorne's place. But the mill in the painting is a lot newer, fancier, too, and the water is bluer than I ever saw it. The mountain in the background is pyramid-shaped, just like Mount

Ascutney across the river, but it's a whole lot taller. Riley says that painting is of some other mill. I'm thinking not. I'm thinking Mr. Parrish just painted scenes how he wanted them to be—not the way they really were. If I were a painter, I'd want to make things look real.

Mrs. Langhorne washes down the pie with tea, strokes the rag rug of hair on her head and says, "When I came up here last fall, I stopped on Route 12-A. I saw the valley, the river and Mount Ascutney in the distance. There was a pine tree off to the left." She pats her mouth with her white napkin and her eyes take on a far-away look. "I knew this is where my picture should live."

I glance around the room, but I don't see the painting. In fact, the walls are bare, and no pictures or knick-knacks are on any of the tables, either. "I'm having the frame restored," she says. "I'm going down to Manhattan next week to pick it up."

I want to ask her who painted it, since I've put plenty of art books away in the 700 section at the library, and even checked out some myself. But Mrs. Langhorne stands up and moves to the window that looks out on the big pine in the driveway. She smiles that little smile again and looks kind of sweet. "Do you think Riley will help me hang it over the mantel?" she asks.

I'd assumed the painting would go on the fancy easel, but Mrs. Langhorne has surprised me again.

"I'm sure Riley will be glad to help you," I say. She nods and rises, heading toward the front door. "Thank you so much for the pie," she says. I know my manners. I know it's time to leave. As I drive back up the hill towards home, I think about what Mrs. Langhorne said. Over the years, lots of folks have found our town special because of the mountain, the river, the trees. Some like the quiet. Some like the space between houses. Not many like the months and months of cold weather. Most of the ritzy folk take long vacations during mud season when it's dreary and wet from melting snow. Plenty of artists and writers have said this is an inspiring place to live, but I never heard anyone say they moved here because they believed it's where a painting should live.

◆◆◆

Riley was replacing some missing shingles on Mrs. Langhorne's roof the day she brought her painting home. She flew out in a heavy river fog that turned the valley to fuzz. Riley was a seaman on an aircraft carrier and knows flying conditions. He can look up into the sky and see fair weather coming when all I see is scud. "Miss Sonia got out and back without a hitch," he says.

So now she's "Miss Sonia." I start to ponder what that means but try to shake it off. He calls all the widow ladies he works for by their first names. There's Miss Anne. Miss Becky. Miss Lorena. Miss

Prudence. Riley says it's a Southern thing he learned from his grandma who grew up near the Smokies in North Carolina.

"Seems like she's a bit old for a Miss," I blurt out, then wish I hadn't.

"I'd say early '60s, no more," Riley says. He cocks his head. "Sixty-one. Yep. For sure." Riley volunteers each year for the town fair, guessing age and weight. He just looks someone over, front, side and back, and knows how old they are and how much they weigh. He's right almost every time. I never have a clue.

I change the subject, getting to what's nagging me. "And what about the painting?"

"Well," he says, "there's a scraggly pine in the front of a valley with some squares—houses I guess—and the mountain beyond looks quite a bit like Mt. Ascutney. There's a high bridge in the background, but it's not covered like our bridge to Vermont. To tell the truth, Clare, that picture looks kind of unfinished if you ask me."

I wonder how much Riley knows about art.

◆◆◆

The Hubbard is still too small to pick from the garden, but I have enough of last year's sweet potatoes in the cellar for a couple of pies. So, the next morning I set to baking then I head back down to Mrs. Langhorne's house just before noon. I'm hoping for a chance to ring the bell, step inside and see the picture over the fireplace. But when I arrive, Mrs. Langhorne is gathering wood from the pile outside the mud room door. I leave the pie on the seat of the car and step out to help her. "You're not lighting a fire today, are you? It's gonna be mid-seventies by afternoon."

"This is for the wood stove, Clare," she says. She picks up two small logs. "I've already brought in two armloads. Just need a couple more after this."

I grab a real load of six logs and follow her inside. "Riley can get you a good deal on a proper new oven," I say. "Last year he put in a new Whirlpool for me. Gas cooktop, too. I don't miss hauling wood and cleaning out the stove pipe. Don't miss the heat the stove gives off in the summer, either."

Mrs. Langhorne puts the two logs on top of the small stack inside the mud room. "I moved up here to get away from those things," she says. "My kitchen in Riverdale had two ovens, a six-burner range and built-in microwave oven. Five bedrooms, six bathrooms, living room, family room, den, finished basement, swimming pool." She smiles. "I had too much stuff, and it wasn't worth anything compared to what I have now. I'm sure I was right, trading that house and a passel of other worthless things for a glimpse of a mountain and a river. That and, of course, my Cezanne. Her lips again rise into a small smile.

"Cezanne?"

"My painting."

I nearly drop the load of wood. Around Christmas I saw on the TV that a picture by that famous French artist sold for—what was it—thirty million dollars? In fact, after seeing that picture on the TV, I made an extra trip down to the library and checked out some books about famous artists, thinking next time I went to the resale store I'd take a closer look at what they had stacked up against the back wall. Plenty of times on *Antiques Roadshow*, folks have picked up something worth a fortune at a yard sale or a resale store. I never did.

Of course, her painting is not the same as the one on the TV. That TV painting was a picture of a blue pot and a bunch of apples sprawling across an old table. But her painting is by that same Frenchman—Mr. Paul Cezanne. And I figure it must be worth ten times—maybe more than ten times— what any one of these big old Colony mansions is worth.

Mrs. Langhorne finally moves aside, and I pile my armload of logs on top of the others. I want to see that picture in the worst way, but Mrs. Langhorne is blocking the door to the kitchen, and I can't peek around her into the sitting room.

"Riley said he hung that picture for you," I say, hoping she'll take the hint. But she just nods. "Your husband is such a help," she says. "That must be a comfort to you."

I wait for her to say more, but she just stands there, her lips a closed-up purse, so I say I only stopped by to check on her and must run off across the river to the Price Chopper. I ask if there's something she needs. She says, "No, but thanks so much for helping me with the logs, and would you please ask Riley to stop over when he has a chance? There's a loose floorboard in the bedroom that needs repairing."

I wonder if the weight of that big sleigh bed in the bedroom hasn't shifted the foundation and loosened a whole bunch of floorboards.

◆◆◆

I go out to the car and wait until Mrs. Langhorne closes the back door. Through the window, I can see her turning towards the sitting room, so I grab the pie off the passenger seat and walk slowly to the front door. When she answers the bell, I tell her I'm sorry, but I forgot to drop off the sweet potato pie. She opens the door wide enough that, even though I'm not invited in, I slip past her and get a glimpse of the painting. There's that pine tree, kind of spindly like a city tree. It's swaying over the top of the mountain. In the valley, there's a bunch of little yellow houses, and here and there little trees. The best part is the purply-pink mountain, almost like Ascutney when the sun hits it on an afternoon in early spring. But overall, like that Maxfield Parrish picture Riley bought me, it doesn't look like anything I've ever seen. I wonder if it's a real mountain, a real valley, a real tree, or if it's something Mr. Paul Cezanne just dreamed up. I wonder how it could be worth the same as a big, fancy house.

While I'm gaping up at her picture, Mrs. Langhorne startles me by putting her hand on my sleeve. She thanks me for coming but doesn't ask me to stay.

◆◆◆

The next day, Saturday, it's not my day to work, but I go across the river and walk into the back door of the library, sneak through the children's section and head for 759.4 where Mr. Cezanne lives. I find him on the middle shelf and open the book. About three quarters of the way through, there's Mrs. Langhorne's picture. It's a little brighter than her painting, but otherwise it's almost the same: the mountain, the swaying pine tree, the valley, the little squares of houses, and, in the distance, a bridge. Actually, it's not a bridge, but more of a trestle, and there seems to be a long train crossing it.

In the book it says that Mr. Cezanne put that painting into an exhibition and his poet friend, Joachim Gasquet, said he liked it. So, what does Mr.

Cezanne do but give him the painting—and paints Gasquet's portrait, to boot. But as soon as Mr. Cezanne died, Mr. Gasquet sold that painting. I guess he didn't like it all that much after all.

According to the book, the painting's now in a museum in London. I want to know a lot more, but they never say as much as you want to know in books with lots of pictures. I'm bamboozled. How did this picture that's supposed to be in a museum come to be sold to Mrs. Langhorne?

I wonder if there could have been another one just like it, or just a little different, or if Mrs. Langhorne was duped. I turn the pages and see another picture of a couple of spindly trees and that same mountain. It says that Mr. Cezanne made some 30 paintings of that mountain—so now I know for sure it's a real place—not something he just made up. I stare at the picture real hard, and the funny thing is, the harder I stare at it, the more real it seems.

But now I'm beginning to worry, thinking that Mrs. Langhorne has paid a huge hunk of money for a fake. I'm up a creek, not knowing what to do. Should I tell Riley? Would he tell Mrs. Langhorne? I decide to think on it for a few days.

◆◆◆

Monday morning, when I'm putting books away in the 595 section—insects, spiders and worms—who do I see but Mrs. Langhorne going down the next aisle. She's already walked past 641, the cooking section, so she's not here to look up recipes for good country pies. She's heading right for 759. I want to rush over and remove the book, so she doesn't find out she's been duped.

I back away and hide in the next aisle over—398, fairy tales. I take a deep breath and peer around the corner. Mrs. Langhorne stops at 759. I'm sure the book is still there since I saw it just two days ago. Folks interested in art usually choose books about our famous colony artists like Maxfield Parrish, Augustus Saint-Gaudens and Frederick Remington. Quite a few folks check out books about Woodrow Wilson, who summered here when he was president. Those books are over in 973. Of course, the books by or about Jerry Salinger are always on the wait list. He's supposed to be a loner, but I see him now and again, lurking about town.

Mrs. Langhorne looks at the top two shelves, backs up, steps aside, bends down and peers at the bottom shelf. Then she runs her finger across the middle shelf, stops and pulls out the very book I looked through on Saturday. I can tell by the cover, a picture of some fellows playing cards. She opens it and begins to turn the pages. I hold my breath. Peek. Hide. Let out my breath. Look again. She's staring at a page in the book. I can't see what page it is, but

I can guess. I hide again, look again. She's reading. She knows.

But the strange thing is, she doesn't let on that anything's wrong. She turns around and sees me watching her. "Why, hello, Clare," she says, a bit too loud. I put my finger to my lips. "Shush," I whisper and take *Grimm's Fairy Tales* out from the shelf. She nods, closes the book and tucks it under her arm. I put Grimm's back where it belongs and watch her head off toward the check-out desk. I'm baffled now for sure.

Maybe she paid someone to steal that painting from the museum. Or maybe she knew it was a fake all along. Maybe the museum sold the painting after that book was published. I sit down on the little stepstool at the end of the aisle and hold my head to keep my brain from spinning. Then, out of the blue, it strikes me that what really happened was that Mr. Cezanne himself copied his own painting of Mount St. Victoire and gave the copy to his poet friend. The original was hidden away somewhere for a hundred years until Mrs. Langhorne bought it at that auction. I'm no detective, but I settle on that explanation because of how it came to me suddenly, like a vision—and because I want it to be true.

◆◆◆

That night, when Riley comes home, he sits down next to me on the swing. He tells me that, when he was fixing Miss Sonia's floor today, she was sitting at that fancy easel, painting trees. "Some fat, some skinny, some kind of wispy and some sturdy, like the pine out her window. You know, she's real good at painting trees."

I look at him, his face in the sunlight tonight bright as new copper. He squints into the dense row of sugar maples.

"What do you see, Riley?" I ask.

He squeezes my shoulder. "I see what I always see," he says, "fresh syrup on my pancakes come spring."

I squint, too. Real hard. At first, all I see are those maple leaves. But then I begin to wonder what Maxfield Parish, Paul Cezanne, Mrs. Langhorne would see. And then I'm thinking how Mrs. Langhorne said she bought a home for a painting. But her river, her mountain, her tree is not the same as Mr. Cezanne's river, mountain, tree. And even if it they were, maybe she wouldn't see them the same way he did.

I lean my head against Riley's shoulder. And as I'm thinking about this place where I've always lived, this place where artists and writers and ritzy folks moved, this place where Mrs. Langhorne moved because of a painting, I notice a purple haze seeping through the trees, like the hidden mountain trickling into view. Then little flecks of gold start showing up among the leaves, like river ice glistening on a winter afternoon. I know what I'm seeing isn't real, but I'm beginning to like the looks of it. I'm beginning to see something that maybe nobody else ever saw in quite the same way. And I'm thinking I like what I'm seeing. I really do.

Sally Stiles

WHAT WILL IMAGINES

My parents moved uptown, from residence to residence, church to church, Greenwich Village to Murray Hill until they bought the condominium off Fifth Avenue. Even that wasn't quite far enough uptown, so in the late '60s, after my grandmother moved to Florida, they took over her big house in Riverdale. My mother lived there a good deal of the time, and my father showed up occasionally, usually on weekends. Though there were other churches closer by, most Sunday mornings they drove half an hour to a well-heeled Episcopal church in

Westchester County. I went with them when I was home, though beginning in ninth grade, that wasn't often.

When I turned fourteen, my father shipped me off to Andrews Academy in Connecticut as a first-year ninth-grade student. I didn't mind. By then I'd been to five private schools and six away-from-home camps and just wanted to stay put in one place. Andrews wasn't a bad place to be. The classes were tough, but I plowed through Latin and a variety of literature, science, social studies and math courses making respectable enough grades to allow me to spend every possible moment on the baseball diamond, basketball court or football field. I was best at baseball and, thanks to my batting skills, bumped the senior first baseman to the bench at the start of my junior year. He was pissed off. I was thrilled.

I was home for a drizzly Easter Sunday that year and was chosen as the crucifer, carrying the big cross and leading the procession down the aisle. Mother took a picture of me standing under the entry eaves of the Westchester church. Since September, I'd grown a full two inches in height and added a couple of inches around my chest, yet my newly shaved cheeks still blushed baby pink. My blond hair was cut in a crew, so short on the sides and on top that it appeared more white than yellow. I was wearing a white-hooded alb tied with a thick cincture.

After my mother took that picture, she kissed me on the cheek and called me by my whole name, as she often did. "William James Langhorne," she said, "make your father proud." That was a tough order.

I looked around for my father and saw him standing at the front door, gesturing to someone next to him in the vestibule. Dad was wearing a three-piece navy suit molded to his five-foot nine, broad-shouldered, 185-pound frame. His bowtie was bright yellow. When I passed him, I touched his sleeve. He turned slightly, nodded and kept on talking to the man I knew to be a partner in one of Manhattan's largest advertising agencies. I was beginning to understand that, for my father, everything—even attending the right church—was a business decision.

He was the son of a dry cleaner in the Bronx and had studied philosophy at NYU. After graduating, he took a trip to Japan and India to study Eastern religions. My mother claims that my father's only enlightenment on that trip was the realization that he didn't want to be poor.

I knew my father as an ambitious man who reveled in the rewards he attained though financial success. I had a harder time figuring out my mother. She'd been a student of art, and told me that, when she was my age, the *Mona Lisa* had changed her life. I often saw her try to imitate that famous, enigmatic smile and wondered what wisdom she concealed behind it.

◆◆◆

My mother followed me inside the church and stood to the side while my father conducted his business. She wore an original white Chanel coat, elbow-length white gloves and a white hat with a broad black band. She carried a matching black and white purse. Finally, my father took her hand, and they sauntered into the narthex, my mother's purse bouncing from its gold chain. They paused to look over the congregation before heading down the aisle, nodding at folks until they reached their pew, up front on the right, the gospel side, just behind the ministers' families. I went downstairs, heading for the room where the acolytes convened.

I don't know why Reverend Joe, the young priest in charge of the acolytes, had given me the honor of carrying the larger of the two gold processional crosses that day. There were plenty of others who showed up every Sunday hoping for the chance. Maybe Reverend Joe chose me because I was an outsider to this group, and he wanted me to feel welcomed. I assumed he didn't realize that I was beginning to question my faith, in large part due to Combat Charlie, the Andrews Academy Modern History teacher and wrestling coach.

Combat Charlie had been incarcerated as a POW in the Hanoi Hilton, and every lesson he taught that year seemed aimed at increasing my awareness of being a privileged white boy who, in order to grow up to be a real man, needed to scrap everything my parents ever gave or taught me. I took on a strong sense of guilt for being the son of a rich man and a woman who seemed to acquiesce to a rich man's yearnings. I began to wonder why I was asked to worship, along with others as privileged as myself, a God that provided—and sustained—a world that thrived on war and meted out pain to those less fortunate than my classmates and me. Still, despite or because of my questioning, I was determined to prove that I deserved the chance to lead the procession down the aisle that day. And, yes, I would make my father proud.

I carried the cross up the back stairs, walked through the vestibule and stood alone in the center of the narthex, waiting for the choir to gather behind me. I held the cross erect, my right palm upward, cradling the shaft, my left hand fully extended and wrapped firmly around it. As the organist played a muted prelude, I looked down the long aisle of red carpet leading to the altar and swayed slightly to the music. Right foot, left.

I watched a younger acolyte, the broad-faced Dye boy, light the paschal candle, then the candles on the altar, first the epistle side, then the gospel side. The last candle on the right didn't catch. It's strange how I remember that—but I remember almost every detail from that extraordinary day. Dye returned to the candle, held the long bronze taper against it until it flickered tentatively, then glowed. The organist paused, turned some pages and began to play soft music again.

I looked over the pews and the extra chairs placed down each side of the aisle. I scanned all the women's wide pink and blue and yellow bonnets until I found the Thorsen family, three quarters of the way down the aisle on the right-hand side. I thought I might be falling in love with Marcie Thorsen and wanted her to turn to look at me, but she was facing the altar, her pink bonnet bowed. Beyond them, in the second row, my mother was twisted fully around, displaying her enigmatic smile. I knew she was counting on me to shepherd the long procession step by careful step down the aisle and usher in a glorious Easter on this disappointingly overcast day. Indeed, the whole congregation seemed unduly hopeful, as if waiting for Jesus himself to miraculously appear—alive, risen from the dead.

When I looked at the bright brass organ pipes behind the pulpit, I recalled a picture I'd once seen. It was taken on the third of June, back in 1941, a rainy day at another church, Christ Church, near our home in Riverdale. In that picture, Babe Ruth stood next to the organ pipes, his head bowed over Lou Gehrig's casket.

I closed my eyes, and the weirdest thing happened. The black and white picture turned to color. A profusion of roses and carnations, brilliant pink and red, surrounded the casket. And then I was in that church—standing in the narthex and looking all the way down the aisle at Babe Ruth, at the flowers, the heavy wooden casket lined in tufted silk and hinged open to reveal Gehrig's face and his folded hands.

Not only was I there, but another man, one who was not in the original picture, stood next to the Babe and looked down at the Iron Horse. His build was similar to mine, but he was a few years older— a sailor. He held his cap in his hand, and his blond hair was cut short like mine. Strangest of all, I knew without question that six months after Lou Gehrig died, that sailor would be on the deck of the *USS Arizona*. On Tuesday, December 7th, 1941, he would sink with the big battleship into Pearl Harbor. He would drown.

If that weren't weird enough, the next thing I knew, I was standing in that sailor's place, as if I were his reincarnation. The sailor was gone, but I was there, smelling the roses and staring down at Lou Gehrig's slicked-back hair, dimpled cheeks and jutting chin.

I shivered and breathed deeply. Had I died at Pearl Harbor to be born again in 1955, sixteen years ago? Was I in Christ Church now? No, I was in Westchester. I'd never even been in Christ Church.

When I opened my eyes, Babe Ruth, the casket and the sailor had all disappeared. Had I fallen asleep standing there? No. I'd had a waking dream, that was all. My imagination had gone on a spree. I shook my head and smiled, thinking sardonically that simply being in church had caused me to make up stuff that wasn't true.

I searched again for Marcie. Her head was raised now, and she seemed to be staring up at the rich stained-glass window over the altar. The window depicted Jesus clutching a shepherd's crook in his left hand and holding a white baby lamb across his right elbow. A flock of lambs beside Him moved forward to cross a small blue stream. Above Jesus, the branches of a tree formed a canopy over a barefoot angel, her wings extended upward, her eyes looking downward, directly at Him. Even on this cloudy day, the light, refracted through dense yellows and whites, deep wine reds and sea blues, was brighter than any natural light.

I stayed fixated on that stained-glass window as I shifted from right foot to left, rehearsing my march down the aisle. To calm myself, I began to recite the 23rd psalm: "The Lord is my shepherd. I shall not want. He leadeth me beside still waters. He restoreth my soul."

But my thoughts were swimming around in my head, refusing to pause long enough to give me a chance to even consider an answer. Soul. What can it really be? Is it something intangible that was born when I was born and lives somewhere deep inside me? I couldn't see it, touch it, photograph it, yet Jesus knew it was there. He knew it needed restoring. "He leadeth me in the path of righteousness"—whatever that path might be. Surely Jesus hadn't led my father down a righteous path to wealth, or my mother to a place where she hid behind her half smile. The path of righteousness couldn't have led Combat Charlie to Vietnam. What about Reverend Joe? Had he found the path by becoming a priest?

If my soul were restored, would it fly to heaven? Or would it find another life? In a baseball star? In a bluebird? In a slimy snail?

◆◆◆

Finally, the members of the choir shuffled into place behind me. The ushers slipped into their seats in the back row. The organ prelude ended on a long, low tone. Then the entire congregation rose, turned and faced me in anticipation of the procession. My mother nodded at me. I nodded back and raised the big cross to its full height. I slid my right foot forward, ready to march.

Reverend Joe moved next to me, his sonorous voice resonating off the high stone vestibule walls.

"He is risen. The Lord is risen indeed.

"This is the day which the Lord hath made; we will rejoice and be glad in it."

The organist began to play the processional. The choir responded: *Christ the Lord is risen today.* And in this instant of joy and expectation, I glanced again at that stained glass window above the altar.

The angel's wings fluttered. Then Jesus moved.

Jesus—alive, alive there in the window— turned his head toward me. He took the lamb from the crook of his arm and held it out to me.

I started, shook my head to clear it and blinked, but Jesus was still holding out that lamb. He was giving me that lamb, as if exchanging its innocent soul for my sinful, privileged, questioning one. I leaned forward and looked at the lamb and then at Jesus' face, at those improbable blue eyes which looked directly into my own eyes. And just then Jesus winked.

I felt the cross slipping sideways in my hand. I flinched and gripped it tighter.

Reverend Joe touched my arm. I'd missed the cue. Right foot, left. I forced myself to move forward into the nave. But with each step I wondered if the bricks beneath the carpet would hold me up, or if I were stumbling through another odd dream. The sopranos pressed behind me, their bright *alleluias* sparkling against the muffled drumming of the basses still back in the narthex. I swallowed, willed myself to keep time with the organ, pounding like my heart. Right, left, right, left. But as I marched closer to the altar, I felt more curious. And I was more afraid. I was afraid that the whole congregation would know that Jesus was judging me.

My mother had said, "Make your father proud." Could she have meant my heavenly father? No. I knew which father she meant. Still, if I continued down the path I was taking and continued to question what the church was teaching, would I fail all of them—mother and both fathers, heavenly and earthly?

My forehead was wet with sweat. I felt hot, then cold, then hot again. I dropped my head, gripped the cross tighter and willed my feet forward. I was three-quarters of the way down the aisle.

I didn't dare look over at Marcie, afraid she'd see me sweating, and, for the same reason, I avoided looking at my mother and father.

I had no idea what had happened. I must have had another weird hallucination. First I'd imagined the sailor, then I'd imagined Jesus winking at me from that stained glass window.

I climbed the steps to the chancel and stood before the altar, head bowed, heart racing while the choir members filed into the stalls just behind me.

They seemed to take forever to reach their seats. Finally, they sang the last *alleluia*. A pause. At last, *amen*. I steadied the cross and climbed the steps, turned left and stopped. I lifted the cross and put it in its stand.

I bowed my head and wiped my forehead against the sleeve of my robe and prayed as hard as I had ever prayed, asking God to stop making me imagine stuff. I'd imagined the sailor. No, he was there, standing right over the casket.

And Jesus had winked. Was it a joke? Jesus' joke? I was just a teenaged kid. Where in the Bible does it say that Jesus messes with kids?

"Jesus," I whispered, "tell me why you winked." No answer. "Jesus, please, tell me that it means that I'm okay with you." No answer.

I wiped the sweat again from my forehead, bowed my head and, once more, prayed. "Okay, Jesus. Just get me through this. Deal with me later if you must, but for now, here in this church, with all these people watching, just get me through this." Again, no answer.

After the sermon, the visiting archdeacon scanned the congregation then climbed down from the pulpit, his white surplice crisp, glasses glinting as if reflecting heaven itself. Before rounding the last step, he turned to gaze at the stained-glass window I'd been avoiding since the service began. I looked up. Jesus' eyes were, again, cast down upon the lamb. Nothing moved.

I looked out at the congregation. The Farmers, all three girls in white dresses, the Franks, the Fitzhughs, Father Joe's pregnant wife, my mother and father, Marcie—all of them were turning the pages of their hymnals. Then they were singing, reading the words in the hymnals and singing. Nobody was noticing anything strange.

So maybe it was all a joke. But Jesus doesn't joke. Maybe it was a joke I played on myself. But that wink. Jesus doesn't wink. Or does he?

♦♦♦

After the service, I met my parents in the parking lot. The chauffeur was off that day, so Dad had driven us to church in his red Eldorado convertible coupe, a floating marshmallow of a car with a preposterously long hood. I'd gotten my driver's license four months before, when I was home over Christmas break, but my father had never let me drive his car. That day he opened the driver-side door and held out the key to me. Had I made him proud? I shook my head and slipped into the back, sinking into the tufted leather seat. I was in no way focused enough to drive.

My father looked at me with some measure of disbelief. Mother looked at me closer and asked if I was feeling okay. I told her I had a headache, the chills. She reached into her purse for an aspirin and handed it to me. I worked up enough saliva to swallow it, then slumped further down in the seat and stayed there while they slipped into a riverfront restaurant for a quick lunch. While they were inside, I tried to replay in my head each time at bat from each baseball game over the previous season in order to stop thinking about what had happened that morning. But I kept seeing a sailor, a lamb, a blue eye winking at me.

♦♦♦

That night I slipped out of the house and snuck my old bike out the side door of the garage. It was drizzling, and I wasn't sure where I was headed, but after meandering past the mansions on Independence Avenue, I found myself riding toward the Henry Hudson Parkway. Before I knew it, I was knocking on the double doors at Christ Church. I turned the brass doorknob, envisioning the dark sanctuary, the silent pipe organ, Babe Ruth, Lou Gehrig's casket, a sailor standing nearby. I leaned against one door, then the other, fell against them, rammed each of them with my shoulder, tried the doorknob again. Nothing budged.

I crept around the church, but even standing on the seat of my bike, the stained-glass windows were too high to reach. I couldn't see inside.

I walked my bike toward the street, then stopped to glance back at the big double doors. They were still firmly closed.

It began to rain hard, pelting me, blurring my vision. I hunkered down and raced home. I took off my wet clothes and collapsed into my bed.

◆◆◆

As I packed to return to school the next morning, I kept shoving everything that had happened the day before into the back of my mind. I'd simply imagined the sailor, the lamb.

But the wink? I held onto that wink. And through the years I recalled it time and time again. And with each recollection, I was a little closer to convincing myself that William James Langhorne, even with all his doubts, had once made Jesus proud.

Sally Stiles

WHAT WILL PONDERS

I back out of our driveway in my new-to-me Pontiac Sunfire, top down, the windows open, turn off Clairmont Road onto Interstate 85, North of Atlanta, and head for New Hampshire, a thousand miles and two days away.

My son, Charlie, sixteen, dials in 96 ROCK to Enigma's "Return to Innocence." I reach for the dial and lower the volume. Charlie looks over at me and grins, turns the sound back up a notch, then pulls his baseball glove out from under the seat. The music swells: *"Just believe in Destiny. Don't care what people say."* Charlie nods to the beat and pounds his fist into the pocket of his glove.

Destiny. I've been thinking about destiny quite a bit of late, mostly because my mother, newly-widowed at age sixty-one, seems to have veered from the road she traveled for four decades with my father. She appears to have found a new, hopefully more satisfying road—one I urged her to take. Since Christmas, she's traveled to France, sold the big house in Riverdale, the condo in New York City, sold or donated most of the furnishings, too. She's bought a place in a remote rural town in New Hampshire. When we've spoken on the phone, she's avoided my questions about the new house. I need to know that she's happy with her move.

The fall semester begins at Emory in a couple of weeks. I teach graduate-level psychology and tend to a few clients in my small private practice. My wife, Elaine, is teaching a summer music appreciation course at Agnes Scott College, and though she can't get away, she's encouraged Charlie and me to take this trip. "When you arrive in New Hampshire," she told me, "I hope you'll be pleased with the mother you find."

◆◆◆

When Charlie was younger, I'd rush home to spend half an hour with him in the back yard, tossing a ball back and forth. On weekends, we'd go to a game or head to Sears for school clothes, hardware or sporting goods, sometimes stopping off at Phidippides at the Ansley Mall to check out the cool athletic shoes. I was determined to be the dad my father couldn't be. But now I'm immersed in teaching college students and helping clients who needed to sort out their lives. Charlie is suddenly interested in dating girls and anxious to win games for his baseball team. So, the summer flew by, and we only went to one Braves game. Not even once did we sneak off to Emory Village after dinner for an ice cream cone.

I yearn for this time together and hope he does, too. The truth is, I was a little surprised that he agreed to come with me since it means he'll miss pitching the last games for his summer league.

When 96 ROCK fades out, Charlie turns the dial. Only one station emerges through the static. A preacher with a thick southern accent alternately damns sinners and praises God. I turn off the radio. Charlie looks out the side window and gently kneads his baseball glove.

Beyond the Atlanta suburbs, we pass fields of parched red clay interspersed with patches of peanuts, cotton, tobacco, soybeans. The landscape is transected from time to time by concrete overpasses, some empty and some thick with traffic. I begin to feel stiff, rotate my neck and stretch my shoulders.

The sun intensifies, so I pull off the highway at the South Carolina Welcome Center, raise the top and turn on the air conditioner.

Back on I-85, Charlie opens up for the first time. He's just seen the movie, *Forrest Gump*. "Dad, when Forrest says that your destiny floats around like a feather on a breeze, do you think it's true? Is everything that happens just random, or does God have some kind of secret plan?"

"There are lots of people who think your destiny is predetermined," I say, "but I have a hard time with that. Why would some folks be sent on a path toward happiness, and some toward disaster?"

"I don't know," Charlie says. "It doesn't seem fair."

"I believe that destiny is accidental to a degree. Think about it. If I hadn't happened to meet your mother at Dooley's, you wouldn't have been you."

Charlie stares into his glove. "Charlie, listen. This is important. I also believe you can make decisions to help shape your destiny."

Charlie smacks his mitt, raises his head and glances over at me. "Like even if you're not too smart—or if you're old like grandma? You can do stuff to change your destiny?"

I feel my shoulders relaxing. This long road trip is going to be better than I expected. "You got it, Charlie."

Charlie tucks the glove under his seat. "There's some weird stuff in *Forrest Gump*," he says. "But I like the part, early on, when Jenny and Forrest are kids, and Jenny asks him if he ever dreams about who he's going to be. His IQ is only seventy-five, so you figure he doesn't have a lot of choices. But Forrest says, 'Who I'm gonna be? Aren't I gonna be me?'"

"You will always be who you are right now," I say. "And you will never stop becoming you." Charlie ducks his head and reaches for the radio dial.

◆◆◆

We're still on I-85 when we approach Charlotte. We skirt around oil tankers, car transporters, double tractor-trailers. I roll down the window to the deep drone of tires on asphalt, to the smell of hot tar and gasoline. I roll the window back up. Malls and housing developments increase in number and size. Billboards and motel signs tower over the trees. I wonder if all the highways in America now look and sound—and even smell—the same.

At Petersburg, Virginia, I turn onto I-95, heading toward Richmond. There's the same flow of trucks, the same motel signs. As the pavement ahead begins to shimmer with late afternoon heat, I wonder if sameness is the American destiny.

Ten hours after we've left home, I pull into a KFC near Ashland and order fried chicken and biscuits from the drive-through. Beyond, a lit vacancy sign flashes against the blue concrete façade of a one-story motel. I raise an eyebrow toward Charlie. He nods. We check in, flop down on the sagging beds and eat the chicken from the bucket. The news on the TV hanging over the scuffed-up dresser is not good news, so I turn it off and fall asleep to the constant flicker of headlights drifting across the pea-green walls of the room.

We're on the road by seven the next morning, passing more trucks, more green highway signs. We skirt DC and Baltimore and head for the New Jersey turnpike where a Wonder Bread truck tailgates us in the passing lane. As I move right into the cruise lane, we're nearly rammed by a Dodge Viper intent on racing across all three lanes to pass us and the truck. "Whoa!" Charlie whispers. "That was close."

"Too damn close," I say. I let out a deep breath.

A mile down the road, the Viper has moved back to the cruise lane and is traveling below the speed limit. I follow a couple of car lengths behind, knowing better than to try to pass him. I look in the rearview mirror. The Wonder Bread truck is, again, tailgating us.

We stop at the Joyce Kilmer service area to take a breather, a bathroom break, to get a cold drink. There is no poetry. There are only a couple of token trees. We don't linger.

◆◆◆

As we get close to New York City, Charlie says he thinks it would be cool to hang out in Manhattan for a while. "Maybe we can do that on another trip," I say. "Your grandmother is expecting us tonight."

"I sure would like to go to Central Park," he says.

I'm surprised. I assume my son would be more interested in going to Yankee Stadium or Madison Square Garden. "Did you know that your grandparents were married in Central Park?" I ask.

"I guess I heard that," Charlie says.

"They were married by a Taoist priest who took them on the carousel after the wedding."

"Really? They rode the merry-go-round in their wedding clothes and all?"

"And your grandmother says your grandfather caught the brass ring."

Charlie laughs and shakes his head. "I'll bet he sold that brass ring to someone waiting in line—sold it for more than it was worth."

I can't help but smile, believing my son is becoming an astute observer of character, though more judgmental than I'd like. "Hey, is that any way to talk about your late grandfather?"

Charlie reaches under his seat for his baseball mitt. "Dad, you know you always told me to tell it like it is."

I know I'm being baited. I let the remark pass.

After crossing the George Washington Bridge, I'm tempted to detour to take a look at our big house in Riverdale. For a few moments I think I'd like to walk down the aisle of the church where, when I was Charlie's age, I thought I saw Jesus wink. But I'm eager to get to New Hampshire. In fact, the closer we get, the more I wonder how my mother is managing in an environment which must be immensely different from the one she left.

I swing the Sunfire onto the Cross-Bronx Expressway, I-95, then take I-91 past Bridgeport, Connecticut, past Springfield, Mass, past rows of cabbage and chard, then apple orchards, pears, the occasional cow. The traffic lets up. I roll down the window and sniff the smell of freshly mowed grass. "That's better," I say. Charlie nods and opens his window, too. I pull into a gas station, fill the tank, roll back the top and let Charlie take the wheel.

We've been on the road eight hours when we finally cross the Connecticut River from Windsor, Vermont, the Sunfire's tires thumping over the expansion joints of America's longest covered bridge.

I tell Charlie to turn left onto New Hampshire Route 12A, then right onto a narrow, winding road. A quarter of a mile beyond, at the top of a rise, I tell Charlie to stop. We stare at a little cottage, lichen growing on the roof. A rusty old Volvo station wagon sits in the driveway.

"This is the right road, and this is the right house number," I say. "But—"

"That definitely doesn't look like any place Grandma ever lived," Charlie says.

When Charlie pulls into the driveway to turn around, my mother bursts out from the front door. I open the passenger-side door. She's laughing, her hands fluttering, strands of mixed gray and brown hair escaping from a bun and trailing down her long neck. "Will! Charlie! You made it. Oh, I'm so glad!"

Mother leads us inside and shows us the guest room where we put our suitcases on folding luggage racks at the end of the twin beds. There's no closet, though a single, unadorned pine chest of drawers faces the beds. The headboards are also pine, also plain, and the beds are covered with blue and white patchwork quilts.

Charlie tosses his glove on the bed, looks out the window at a scruffy patch of overgrown garden, then at me as I pull my black leather toiletry kit from my suitcase. "Dad, I thought Grandpa was really rich. Didn't he leave Grandma any money? Why is she living in this little house?"

I've seen the trust papers and know my mother inherited plenty. And, though Charlie hasn't been told, when he turns twenty-five, he will be well on his way to becoming a millionaire. Knowing that sudden money can send a life off on a troubled path,

I've already rehearsed the talks I plan to have with my son before his twenty-fifth birthday.

"Your grandpa left your grandma very well off," I say. "But there are things more important than money, right?"

"Yeah, I guess that's true," Charlie says. He pulls a book out from his suitcase, sits on the edge of the bed facing the window and begins to read.

I'm stacking my underwear, jeans and polo shirts in the bottom drawer of the dresser but stop when I notice the painting on the wall between the two beds. I'm certain I've never seen it before. Storm clouds gather over the left side of a blue-gray mountain, partially obscured by a dark green pine tree. The right side of the painting is lighter, with yellow tones, giving the impression that the afternoon sun is pushing back the rain. The signature at the bottom appears to be Sonia Langhorne—my mother. I know mother once studied art at Pratt, but I've never seen her hold a brush in her hand.

After emptying my suitcase, I step into the sitting room. There, hanging over the fireplace, is another painting. Again, there's a mountain and, again, in the foreground, a pine tree—or, rather, a thin and graceful impression of a pine tree, with long branches mirroring the sweep of the mountain. I've seen this painting before but can't remember where or when. It wasn't in the house in Riverdale or in the condo in Manhattan.

"Mother," I say, "this painting. Where?—"

"I bought it on a whim in Marseilles." She takes me by the hand and leads me toward the kitchen. I look back at the painting, but she turns my head toward her. "You must be hungry."

I shake my head. "Not much, but Charlie's always hungry."

"I suspected so. I've got shepherd's pie in the oven. Come help me serve it up."

That night, after Mother has closed her bedroom door, I step quietly into the sitting room. I turn on the lamp next to the blue couch and inspect the painting over the fireplace. I've seen that mountain before—in a book or maybe in a museum, a painting by Paul Cezanne. I look closely at the signature: *P. Cezanne*. I look again. I'm stunned. I have no idea how Mother managed to acquire this masterpiece. I fall back on the couch and take it in: the mountain in the distance, the pine branch sweeping across the foreground, the houses, the bridge. I'm beginning to understand that, indeed, my mother has exchanged the trappings of her New York life for something she believes to be more valuable.

By the front window is an ornate wooden easel, the easel that always stood in the corner of the formal living room in the house in Riverdale. My mother's portrait used to sit on that easel, but it's gone, and nothing has replaced it. I smile. I hope that Mother works at that easel—that it and the painting over the mantel represent her return to a long-abandoned path.

I've counseled enough clients her age to know that approaching age sixty-five can lead to despair over losing a long-established identity. Or, the sixties can be a time of transformation, of reclaiming lost dreams. Is it possible that my mother is actually rediscovering the person she was before she married my father? Is she painting a new destiny?

I rise from the couch, turn out the light and slip into the guest room. Charlie is asleep, his mouth slightly open, his left arm flung over a book. I carefully slide the book out from under Charlie's arm and read the title: *Shoeless Joe.* There's a ghostly picture of a baseball player on the cover. I put the book on the bedside table and turn off the light.

When I sink into the mattress, I realize I haven't felt this content in a long, long time.

WHAT CHARLIE WANTS

Grandma has moved from New York all the way up to New Hampshire. She's living in a little cottage, so different from the condo in the city or the big place in Riverdale. Grandma seems a little different, too. In the city, she'd serve us a store-bought cheesecake for dessert, but today we're finishing up a homemade Hubbard squash pie. It doesn't taste like squash to me—and it's a whole lot better than cheesecake.

I'm leaning back in my chair, rubbing the big A on my Braves shirt, when I notice Grandma staring at me. Immediately I sit upright and thank her for the lunch, the pie. She's still staring at me. "Grandma?"

"I'm sorry, Charlie. I was just thinking about how much you resemble your dad at sixteen— except for your eyes. You have your grandfather Logan's eyes—deep amber."

I get a little depressed when Grandma talks about Grandpa, who died last year. I never know what to say. But there's something else I really want to find out, so I just blurt it out. "Uh, Grandma, I was wondering if you've met anyone interesting yet."

"I'm just getting to know some folks who seem interesting enough," she says.

I nod in the direction of the hill up from Grandma's house. "What about that famous writer guy who lives up there? You seen him yet?"

"Jerry's pretty reclusive," she says.

I'm surprised that she calls him by his first name. "Do you know him?" I ask.

"Not really," Grandma says. "But when I found out he was living here, I started to read his books again, figuring I should, in case he ever comes up in conversation."

She looks right at me again. "Charlie, how did you know he lives close by?"

I don't want to let on too much, so I just tell her it was something the school librarian mentioned. Dad cocks his head, like he's surprised, but he doesn't say anything.

Grandma pushes her pie plate aside and starts to rise but sits back down in her chair. She hesitates, looks out the window toward the big pine tree in the front yard, then back at me. "Have you read his books?"

"Well—"

"All of them?"

"Only the *Catcher* book and, well, some of the stories," I tell her. "I like *Catcher* better."

"The people he writes about seem both exaggerated and real, both flawed and benevolent," she says. "What do you think?"

"I think they're real. At least Holden is real. And he cares—he really cares about, well, his brother Allie, who died, and Phoebe and the ducks in Central Park and all. And, Grandma, isn't it pretty cool that Holden tells it like he sees it and wants to catch the children before they fall over the cliff?"

Grandma is leaning back in her chair with her eyes closed. I wonder if she's okay.

"Grandma?"

She opens her eyes and shakes her head like she's just waking up and says she's thinking about Holden taking Phoebe to Central Park. She says the day she and Grandpa were married, he caught the brass ring on the carousel. "He kept the free ticket he'd won, saying we'd use it when our first child was old enough to ride. The ticket was still in his wallet when he died."

I look at Dad, thinking he'll be really sorry to hear that his father never gave that free ride to him. Dad just shrugs his shoulders. "I never lacked for merry-go-round rides," he says.

Grandma clears her throat and stands up, looking down at me, then says, "Actually, Charlie, there's not a character in any of Jerry's books who doesn't leave me a bit despondent."

"A lot of books are sad," I say.

"Yes. A lot of life is—"

I'm thinking she's going to say, "sad", but instead she smiles a brave little smile, stacks her plates and heads to the kitchen.

◆◆◆

Dad asks me to help him clean up the dishes. He rubs a scrubber over the pie pan and says, "So, you've been thinking you might run into Salinger here?"

"Well, it is a small town," I say.

Dad rinses the soap from the pie pan and hands it to me to dry. When he speaks again, I feel that he's talking to the overgrown garden outside the window over the sink rather than to me.

"I've read all of Salinger's books. There's some pretty perplexing stuff in them. I'm still not sure why firing a bullet through your right temple might be an appropriate response to war," he says. "But I think it's important to shine your shoes, to do your best for Seymour's Fat Lady, whether she's the ugly woman in the audience or Christ himself."

He soaps the glasses. "You know, Charlie, I once thought Jesus—" He takes a deep breath, shakes his head and begins to rinse the glasses in clean water. He hands them to me, one by one and says, "there's a lot of poetry in Salinger's books. Seymour has a passion for haiku. He's written, what, 184 unpublished poems?"

As he hands me the last glass, I'm still trying to sort out what he's trying to tell me. Then he looks at me intently. "And there's Allie's left-handed fielder's mitt, full of poems in green ink."

Now he's talking to me. "I wish he'd written out some of those poems," I say. "I keep wondering what they said."

In fact, I wanted to copy one of Allie's poems on my own baseball glove but couldn't find one in the book. The guys on the team would probably laugh at me, but I still want to write something— something important to think about between pitches, something like Allie might have written. I've even bought a felt Sharpie with green ink, but I can't figure out what to say.

Dad grabs a handful of silverware soaking in a bowl. He hesitates, then looks at me again. "Son, do you understand that Holden is mourning the innocent childhood he lost? That he distains the phony world he entered when his little brother, Allie, died? Did you figure out that Holden wants to catch the children before they lose their innocence?"

"I guess so, Dad. I was pretty sure he wanted to keep them safe."

As I dry the knives, forks and spoons, then look around for the silverware drawer, I wonder why growing up and losing your innocence is so bad.

◆◆◆

When we're done with the dishes, I grab my baseball mitt and ball and ask Dad if he wants to play a little catch. Dad agrees, but he says he doesn't have a glove. I hand him mine.

In the yard, I pace off sixty feet and throw Dad a perfect fastball. It lands in the pocket of the glove. Dad tosses the ball back, and I repeat the pitch. Again, Dad catches it. "Good job, Dad."

After a dozen more pitches, I throw a slider, which breaks away when Dad reaches for it. The ball skitters past the big pine tree in the yard.

I run over to retrieve the ball and stop, looking up the road.

Dad comes over to me and hands me my glove. "What is it, son?"

I realize I'm stroking the glove against my hip. I stop and look at Dad. "I was just thinking about

Shoeless Joe, this really neat book I'm reading."
Dad nods.

"So, what happens is that the author, Ray
Kinsella, pulls into the guy's driveway." I swallow
then call him by his first name, the name Grandma
used. "So, Kinsella pulls into Jerry's driveway—and
hangs out there until the Jeep shows up."

"Go on, Charlie."

"Well, then Kinsella gets out of his car. He
sticks his finger through the pocket of his jacket, like
he's packing a pistol, and when the old guy, Jerry,
who doesn't want anyone bothering him, gets out of
the jeep, Kinsella tells him the only reason he's
kidnapping him is to take him to a baseball game—
which happens to be in Boston. I sure would like to
meet that guy."

Dad grins. "Which guy? Kinsella? Or Shoeless
Joe?"

"Hey, Dad, don't tease me. You know I mean
the other guy, the one who lives up there beyond the
top of the hill. Jerry. The guy Kinsella kidnapped. In
the book, he turned out to be a really cool dude."

"So," Dad says, "you're going to hide in Mr.
Salinger's driveway, pretend you have a gun and
kidnap him? Take him to Boston?"

"Oh, Dad, that would be epic. But all I really
want—"

"Charlie, I think the man is living here because
he doesn't want to be bothered."

"I just want to see him, that's all." But there's more. I believe that if I could just talk to him, he'd tell me something important, and I could write what he says on my baseball glove.

◆◆◆

Later that afternoon, we're all supposed to go over to the Saint-Gaudens National Historic Site, the home of the famous sculptor who lived just around the corner from Grandma's cottage. At the last minute, I tell them I want to stay and finish reading *Shoeless Joe*. Dad starts up the Sunfire and rolls back the top. Grandma gets into the passenger seat, and they take off.

I sit in one of the Adirondack chairs under the big pine in front of the cottage and look up at the mountain across the river. In a few minutes I get up and begin to trot up the hill. I turn right onto Lang Road then left onto an unpaved road and stand looking at an angular gray house overpowered by large second-story dormer windows. Next to the house is a barn-like garage. I'm sure it's his place, so I walk slowly up the side of the driveway and approach the front door, then take a deep breath and ring the bell. My heart is racing.

I ring the bell again. A tall, white-haired man with large, dark eyes opens the door. His high forehead is furrowed, his thick white eyebrows drawn together. He looks thin, tired, sad—not the way I imagined he would look.

"I'm not the answer to your question," he says. His voice is both kind and firm. He shuts the door.

I backtrack down the walkway and squat under the deck to the side of the house. I tell myself that Dad was right. I shouldn't have bothered the poor guy, all spent out, maybe done with writing, maybe done with life.

Then I hear a soft voice in my head, a voice that sounds a little like my father's voice, but the words are the same words Ray Kinsella heard in his head before kidnapping Jerry in *Shoeless Joe*. I hear the voice again, this time insistently: "*Ease his pain.*"

I start down the driveway, trying to think of a way to ease Jerry's pain. I can't kidnap him; can't take him to Boston; can't even talk to him. I wonder if I could leave a letter at his door, a note that would make Jerry happy. That's nuts. I can't even write something meaningful on my own baseball glove.

Then another idea occurs to me. I race down the hill, run into the guest room and grab my glove off the pillow. I find the green felt pen at the bottom of my suitcase and trudge back up to the gray house. I'm thinking it might ease Jerry's pain to write out one of Allie's poems—to make Allie live again. And then I'm thinking how cool it would be if Jerry wrote a whole bunch of Allie's poems all over my glove.

I stand to the side of the door, place my baseball glove and the green felt-tip pen on the step, ring the bell and crouch behind the bushes. I hear the door open and see a long shadow reach down and slowly rise back up. If Jerry steps outside the stoop and spots me, I could be in big trouble. I hunker further down beneath a thorny bush and hold my breath.

Jerry's long shadow doesn't move, and I'm beginning to feel that I've made a huge mistake. Maybe Jerry will write "Good Luck" across my mitt, words as meaningless to me as to Holden. Even worse, he'll write, "Fuck You!" like someone wrote on the wall at Phoebe's school. It drove Holden nuts.

What if Jerry filches the glove and the pen and won't give them back? I've been kneading that glove, shaping the pocket, for almost a year. That glove took me and my team to third place in the state championship.

Maybe I should just grab the glove and run, but I force myself to stay crouched under the bush. Finally, the shadow recedes. The door clicks shut. Still, I stay hunkered down and count to sixty before peering around the corner. I'm relieved to find my glove sitting on the step. Something is written in small letters in green ink just below the web. I reach over, snatch the glove and the pen beside it, slip back behind the bush, creep along the side of the house and race down the driveway.

It's not until I'm halfway down Lang Road that I stop, duck behind a maple tree, breathe in deeply, exhale, turn the glove over and read what Jerry has written:

hidden beneath
my Bittersweet bush
a seedling poem

A Bittersweet bush, a seedling, a poem. What does that have to do with life, with baseball? With me?

I read it again, slowly now, adding words. He saw me beneath his bush, both bitter and sweet. Like life. Okay. I get that. And he imagined a seedling—not just any seedling—a seedling poem—an idea, a beginning, a possibility. A possibility. An opportunity—just like every pitch, every game, every poem, every book ever written. Every day. Every life—mine, Dad's, Jerry's, even Grandma's. Possibilities. So many possibilities. "Yes!"

I look back at Jerry's house. "Yes!" I shout. "Yes! Yes! Yes!" I wave my glove over my head and take off running down the hill.

Sally Stiles

WHAT SONIA DISCOVERS

My only child and grandchild descend the hill toward the highway in their '93 red Sunfire, the top down. The car slows and my son, Will, leans out of the driver's side. He twists around, smiles, waves goodbye. Then my 16-year-old grandson, Charlie, raises his baseball mitt and whirls it high above his head.

Before they left, Charlie showed me the mitt, the writing in green ink beneath the web. To my amazement, my grandson tracked down the reclusive writer who lives half a mile up the hill. The townspeople keep his address a secret from prying fans and the press, and I'm not even sure which house is his. But Charlie knew. Even more to my amazement, Salinger, whom I've only glimpsed scowling outside the general store, wrote three lines on Charlie's glove.

> *hidden beneath*
> *my Bittersweet bush*
> *a seedling poem*

I can imagine Charlie growing into a poem—perhaps a heroic poem, an epic, free verse, or perhaps—my preference, maybe Salinger's, too—a gentle haiku.

Even after the Sunfire disappears onto the highway, I stand there by the mailbox, reluctant to return to my empty house. For a fleeting moment, I wish I had ignored Will's advice and moved to Atlanta where he and his family have settled.

I wonder if I didn't mess up my last forty years by dropping out of Pratt to marry Logan, then allowing him to lead me rung by rung up the New York social ladder. When I moved to this little cottage, I felt it right to sell or donate almost everything we had acquired during our nearly forty years of marriage. Was I furious with Logan for dying, for leaving me alone? Or was I furious with myself for having allowed him to control forty years of my life? Maybe both—or neither—are true. At any rate, it no longer matters. What matters now is the path I take forward.

If I were a seedling, would I be weeded out from under a Bittersweet bush and tossed aside? Or would I find the nourishment I need to re-root, to thrive in a new location?

◆◆◆

Until a few months ago, I'd always lived within ten miles of Manhattan. What do I know about life in the countryside? When I wake up in the middle of the night, I'm still surprised to see no lights shining through the window, to hear no sounds of traffic, horns, ambulances. Often there's a creak, a squawk, a faint tapping sound, so I check the doors then lie awake, listening until the sound disappears, or until sleep wins out over my fear.

With my son's encouragement, I made the decision to move here to be free to pursue my own yearnings. And I am free, absolutely free. I can make friends with people who interest me, find new paths to follow. I can paint what I like, though at sixty-one, I wonder what I have to offer. I'm no Grandma Moses.

◆◆◆

I'm still standing at the edge of the driveway long after Will and Charlie have turned onto the highway. I'm not ready to return to my cottage, not ready for the solitary sound of one set of footsteps on the wide pine floors. I flip open my mailbox, figuring it will be empty, and it is, so I turn and walk up the hill, stopping at the bridge over the Blow Me Down brook. Beaver have created a log dam just upstream. The pond above their dam extends shore to shore, and, in the center, a rough pile of logs and sticks must provide a place for the beavers to escape predators when winter comes.

And winter is coming soon enough. Will my wood stove and fireplace create sufficient heat? Will I be snowed in? Will I have enough firewood to last through the long months? I'd always begged Logan for some quiet time during the holidays. Will Thanksgiving, Christmas, and New Year's Eve be painfully quiet this year?

I turn back toward my house but, once more, change direction, traveling down a path that I didn't anticipate. I walk down the highway past the small stone and shingle building that was once a grist mill. A steady sheet of water spills from the mill pond into the brook below. Beyond the pond, I enter the woods leading up the hill to Aspet, a National Historic Site, the former home of sculptor Augustus Saint-Gaudens. Yesterday, Will and I wandered through the house and admired Saint-Gaudens' work on display in the Little Studio. There's more I want to see.

The trail is narrow and steep. I stop halfway up, feeling the calm, the lack of wind—no rustling leaves or whispering pine needles. I step over tree roots and avoid low ferns growing on both sides of the path. A Junco whistles overhead. I pause to listen. Then, before I expect it, I arrive at a meadow. Beyond is a broad expanse of clipped grass surrounding Saint-Gaudens' large white Federal-style brick home. There are outbuildings and precisely-trimmed pine hedgerows, some oblong and some circular, which portion off sections of the grounds and buildings. A profusion of old vines hangs from the wrap-around portico. Across the Connecticut River valley, Mount Ascutney rises through a clear blue sky, its pyramid peak resting on broad shoulders.

I picture the scene as it was 1890, when Saint-Gaudens was living at Aspet. Carriage horses are being led from the barn. A man in overalls is pushing a tiller along a terrace below the house. Mrs. Saint-Gaudens is tending a bed of purple and pink hollyhocks. Neighbors arrive in tweed jackets and knickerbockers for an afternoon of lawn bowling on the manicured green or for a round of golf on the little course which meandered through the property.

I recall a picture of the buildings, the meadows, the statuary, the mountain beyond covered in deep snow. Apprentices and studio workers are lined up for a turn on the toboggan run. When I breathe deeply, I conjure up the smell of wood smoke. I listen for the faint sound of a sonata coming from the Fisher piano within the house.

◆◆◆

A rustling in the tall grass brings me back to the present. A fox raises its head and stops to look at me before scampering off into the woods. I skirt the Temple, a marble monument which houses the Saint-Gaudens family ashes, pass a row of apple trees, the fruit beginning to form on the carefully-pruned branches, then stroll the grounds until I find a gap in the hedgerow surrounding the bowling green.

I feel as if I'm entering holy ground. At the far end is a massive relief in bronze. The center figure is a tall rider reining in a determined horse. I recognize the uniform: Union Army, Civil War. The men marching beside the rider are all African American—old and young, steadfast, able, noble. Each man leans forward—purposeful, resolute—in step with the drummer boy ahead. Regiment Fifty-Four.

I've seen the original of this monument at Beacon and Park Streets in Boston and know the memorial commemorates young Colonel Robert Shaw and his regiment of 600 Union soldiers heading South from Boston during the Civil War.

They led the assault on Fort Wagner, the approach to Charleston Harbor. Colonel Shaw and nearly half of his men were killed at Fort Wagner. I yearn for the story to end differently—to end in triumph.

As I approach the sculpture, I want to touch the faces, stroke the bedrolls which, though bronze, appear as soft as fabric. I want to join the soldiers on their march. I want to acquire a measure of their courage. I look at each soldier in turn, then look again, wanting to memorize their faces.

After leaving the green, I walk toward the formal garden. There's another opening in the hedgerow, and I move slowly, softly, as I feel I must, approaching the Adams Memorial. The bronze figure, fully draped by a shroud created from a thin sheet of bronze, is seated on a rock and leaning against a thick slab of polished granite. The eyes are closed. The chin rests on the right hand.

The features remind me of a classical Roman sculpture: the extended neck, straight nose, quiet, full closed lips. I've seen pictures of this monument, the original in a cemetery in Washington, D.C. It's a bronze funerary for Marian Hooper Adams—called Clover—a socialite and photographer, the wife of historian and author Henry Adams. But the face is not Clover's. At Henry Adams' request, Saint-Gaudens crafted an androgynous, inscrutable face, a portrait of meditation. Clover committed suicide.

I ponder the sculpture for a good while, examining the features, the hand reaching up to cradle the chin. I find myself transfixed by the mixture of realism and idealism, the sheer brilliance in its simplicity. I move from side to side, then nearer to the figure. I look up at her closed eyes and close mine as well. I no longer feel a sense of melancholy. Reflection, perhaps. Contentment. Even peace. I open my eyes and—yes—the memorial represents someone at peace—just as Henry Adams must have wished.

As I leave, I hear music rising from the lawn beside the Little Studio. It's the lyrical, pensive second movement of Schubert's String Quartet #14. The music's tempo and intensity will increase; it will end in the fourth movement with wild, tumultuous harmonics, a demonic tarantella. I have always been troubled—no, alarmed—by the ending to this quartet, and today, especially, when I am looking for assurance, I'm in no mood for Schubert's pessimistic rage.

I hasten toward the Ravine Trail then slip into the studio nestled against the white pine trees. Inside, a tall man who appears to be in his late twenties, wearing jeans and a black turtleneck, is bent over a clay model of a young woman's head. The model's eyes are wide open, her expression one of awe, her hair naturally windblown, as the sculptor's hair appears to be. He glances up and says, "Hi, I'm Benno."

I'm startled by the sculptor's amber eyes, nearly the color of my late husband's eyes, the color of my grandson's eyes, though the sculptor's earnest, steadfast gaze reminds me more of my grandson, Charlie.

While Benno works, he tells me that the clay figure he's creating will go through a long and complex process to eventually become a bronze. I ask him to tell me more.

"The clay must be finished, smoothed and dried," he says. He applies a small tool, a loop tool, he calls it, above the right eyebrow. "When she's finished to my satisfaction, maybe tomorrow, she'll be coated—several times—with rubber to form a mold. Then the rubber is coated with plaster."

I tell him that she's already beautiful. "She looks like she's just setting off on a grand adventure—a lifetime of discovery."

Benno smiles and picks up another tool from the assortment on the sculpting table. He lifts a strand of the figure's hair and shifts it slightly higher, then pauses to inspect the model before he speaks again. "When the rubber and clay are removed, the plaster remains. It becomes the mother mold."

I move a step closer. "May I ask—is she someone you know?"

Benno puts down his tool, stands up and stretches. He scratches the back of his neck, then strokes the deep cleft of his chin. "She's someone I want to know," he says.

Again, I admire the windblown hair, the look of awe. I wonder if I might have once resembled that girl.

Benno rubs his finger over a spot behind the figure's ear and continues: "The plaster mother mold is filled with hot wax. When the wax has hardened, the plaster is carefully removed."

I imagine that Benno has explained the lost-wax process to visitors a hundred times over, but his voice is gentle, patient. He stands up, wipes his finger on his jeans and says, "The wax impression is dipped into slurry which creates a hard ceramic shell. The shell is heated, the wax flows out and melted bronze poured in to replace the wax. Then the shell is hammered away to reveal the bronze."

I can visualize Benno's clay figure as a finished bronze, a perpetual reminder of a woman still in her youth, a woman whom I believe Benno will come to know. Perhaps he will model her many times, sculpting the transformations in her face, her hair, her expression—capturing her changing essence through the years. How many times will she be coated, recoated, filled, emptied, filled again, another shell hammered away, another exquisite bronze revealed?

Benno clears his throat. "Do you have any questions?"

"I had no idea there were so many stages. Is the bronze then finished when the shell is removed?"

"Not quite," he says. "The metal chaser at a foundry removes imperfections. If the sculpture is large, it can consist of many molds, which are then welded together, and the weld lines are chased away. The finished piece is sandblasted to make it smooth, and it glows like gold."

He walks toward a bench, hefts a bronze head, one that resembles a soldier in the Shaw memorial. He brings it closer to me. "See how the eyes are darkened, the cheeks highlighted? Chemicals have been applied to create the patina.

"If we have the mother mold," he adds, "we can reproduce this bronze. We start with pouring wax into the mold, then go through the process again." He smiles broadly, kindly, as he replaces the figure on the bench.

"When I look at Saint-Gaudens' work, Benno says, "it reminds me of something George Bernard Shaw once said. 'You use a glass mirror to see your face; you use works of art to see your soul.'"

I tell him that I already see something of my soul in his young woman.

Benno says that he's just a beginner, but he believes he has found his calling. I believe Benno has discovered more than a calling. I believe he has discovered love—love for his work and, perhaps, for a young woman with wind-blown hair, a woman who will become even more intriguing through the years.

On leaving the studio, I hear the last ferocious chord of Schubert's quartet, then muffled applause, mere background to my pondering. I slip into the woods, still marveling at the complex process of creating a bronze—from concept to drawings to clay to mother mold to wax to metal to patina—each careful step required to create a sculpture that will reveal souls long after I am gone; after my son, Will, his son, Charlie, and even Charlie's children are gone.

WHAT CLARE WINS

It's noon before I've finished my chores and take off for the town fair. As I pass through the gate, I'm thinking that a hot dog topped off with mustard and onions and flushed down with an orange slush would do me just fine. I'll wait 'til later for the candy apple.

I stroll through the midway, licking mustard off my fingers, and pause to watch the games of chance. Kids and their dads squirt water pistols, shoot rifles, hurl darts and baseballs, none of which seem to hit close to a target. One tall teenager tosses a basketball that skitters around the rim but falls away from the hoop. The carney barker, who's wearing a sleeveless muscle shirt, flexes his arms so that mermaid tattoos swim across both biceps. He swoops up the ball and holds it out to the young fellow. "I know your sweetheart wants one of them pink teddy bears. Give it another shot, Lover Boy." The girl with a ponytail and turned-up nose standing next to him nods and hands the carney man a dollar. The boy holds the ball with both hands, squints up at the rim, ready to shoot—then stops, turns and hands the girl the ball. Her shot misses the rim entirely. He takes her hand and pulls her away.

The carney man hollers after them: "Hey, Lover Boy. This is your lucky day! I'll give you two more chances for a dollar." The girl stands on her tiptoes to whisper something to the boy. He nods, and they walk back to the booth. He pulls a dollar from his wallet. Since I don't want to watch that dollar wasted, I move on.

I spot my husband's booth with his big scale and a sign: *Stump Riley and Win!* Riley doesn't charge folks anything for guessing their age and weight. If he's wrong, which isn't often, he hands them a ticket for a free cotton candy. If he's right, he asks them to put a dollar in the pot for the rescue squad. A good many of them slip in a five. Last year Riley handed the selectmen a stack of bills near a foot high. This year he's aiming for a two-foot stack.

A dozen folks are waiting in line behind a woman with skinny legs and a monster bust. She steps up to the platform next to the scale. While she seems to be about my age, on the far side of forty, she's dressed like a teenager in a frilly top, tight cut-off jeans and white cowboy boots. Her hair is streaked yellow and puffed up high. I'm thinking she's got two pounds of hair, a pound of boots. I can't even begin to imagine the weight of what's bouncing inside her bra.

Riley asks her to turn around. I watch him closely, but his eyes don't linger anywhere they shouldn't. He writes her name, Dolly, on the chalkboard then holds up the board so the crowd can see him filling in the numbers.

DOLLY
AGE: 47
WEIGHT: 132

Most of the folks standing in line smile and nod, but one scrawny white-haired lady stomps her cane in the dirt and scowls. I'm thinking she's wishing she was still 47 and weighed as much as 132.

Riley holds the mike out to Dolly and asks her to say her true age. Dolly shuts her eyes and whispers into the mike: "Forty-seven, but don't tell anyone." The crowd laughs.

Riley tells Dolly to step up on the scale. The arrow spins up and stops two notches above 130. Folks begin to clap. Even the white-haired lady smiles. Dolly pulls a dollar out from her blouse and hands it to Riley. She starts to step off the platform, but stops, digs into her ruffled pink fanny pack and drops a couple of more bills in the big black pot.

Riley tips his pork pie hat and says, "Thank you kindly, ma'am."

I cut to the front of the line and reach up to give Riley a pat on the knee.

"That's my wife," he says. "She won't tell me how old she is, and her weight is a secret—even to me." The crowd laughs again. I check the pot. The bottom is already covered with dollar bills. I tell him I'll be back in a little while.

◆◆◆

The good stuff is beyond the midway—past the Ferris wheel, tilt-a-wheel, Zipper and Orbiter where folks are spun around, their arms and legs a-flying. You wouldn't catch me on such a wobbly contraption. Off to the side, in the children's section, a bunch of giggling little ones are riding the merry-go-round, but they're seated on cars and motorcycles, not on horses that rise up and down like they did back in my day.

A bunch of boys, age eight or nine, race across in front of me. Two of them, their faces painted to look like tigers, are sharing caramel corn, laughing and swinging a stuffed purple monkey between them.

I give a wide berth to the guy tossing around a big yellow snake, its red-forked tongue darting in and out. Just beyond are the fenced-off dirt rings where they hold the oxen pulls and tractor pulls, the horse pulls, axe-throwing and lumber cutting competitions. I see two Clydesdales being led to a sleigh loaded down with cement blocks. Billy and Tommy Trumbly, brothers from the Flat, hook the horses to the sleigh, and right off, the Clydesdales start straining like crazy, moving forward foot by foot.

A dozen folks lean on the fence and cheer them on. Billy waves his orange Town Line Equipment ballcap and smiles while Tommy unhooks the horses. A forklift attached to an orange tractor picks up another stack of blocks and adds them to the sleigh. The brothers hook the horses up to the heavier load and grab the reins. I'm happy for Billy and Tommy, having a chance to show off their strong work horses, but I don't want to watch those poor Clydesdales strain even harder.

I walk past the entertainment stage and the wee-wee pig-racing track to reach the barns where all the 4-H youngsters are grooming their cows, horses and sheep. Some of 'em are mucking out the stalls and others tossing in pitch forks full of fresh hay. Outside, two sheep are being held in halters while being sheared. I watch the children working and feel good knowing there are still kids serious about tending to their animals.

Riley and I don't have the acreage for cows and such, but ten years ago, when they were twelve, our twins, Harry and Gary, won a blue ribbon for the eggs that their hens, Mary and Carrie, hatched. The boys hung that ribbon over the coop and smiled each time they passed it. That winter, Macho Mike, their rooster, got snatched up by a fox. That's when our boys decided they'd done enough chicken raising.

◆◆◆

What I really want to see is in the school building, just beyond. As I enter, a girl is bounding down the hall toward me. She's wearing horn-rimmed glasses, a tiara, and a white ribbon is draped across her chest. She waves at me and, as she skips by, she calls out, "Hi, Aunt Clare." Only then do I realize that she's Riley's sister's baby girl, Lisa, all grown up now, wearing lipstick, a sleeveless blue lace dress and, according to the words on that ribbon, she's been chosen as queen of the fair.

Back when I was her age, I filled out an application for the queen contest and asked my mother for the entry fee, but she said it was a silly contest and, anyway, you needed to be pretty and smart and talented to win. She didn't say I *wasn't* pretty, smart or talented, but she sure didn't say I was. The girl who won that year was kind of boney and had crooked teeth, but she did seem smart enough. She played the guitar and sang cowboy songs—and, boy, could she ever yodel! Even better than Gene Autry. I can hear her now: *yodel-ay-ee-oooo.*

When my boys were in grammar school, I tried to get them to enter the contest to be chosen princes of the fair. I was pretty sure my handsome twins would win, but they said the contest was for sissies. I've always believed they didn't enter 'cause they were afraid they wouldn't win.

♦♦♦

It's stuffy and strangely quiet in the school building. The hallway is dim, but I follow an arrow to a classroom. Desks have been stacked against the back wall, and the room is filled with shoved-together tables covered with ironed tablecloths. On the tables are displays of fruit and vegetables, jams, bread, cupcakes and pies.

I head right for the pies. There are a lot of entries this year—all smooth-looking crusts, some latticed, some perfectly pinched to the edges, no fillings leaking out. There's blueberry, huckleberry, peach and apple pies, each with a little slice removed where the judge has taken a taste. I see a red ribbon on Suzie Lamb's cherry pie. I'm not surprised. Suzie always wins something at the fair. Her husband's a chef at the Windsor Station restaurant across the river. I think he actually bakes her pies.

I look and look but can't find my Hubbard squash pie. Then, at the table just behind me, I see Riley's new handyman customer, Mrs. Sonia Langhorne. I'm surprised she's here since she knows nothing about baking, though she says she's fond of what she calls my "good country pies."

She waves at me, then smiles and calls out, "Congratulations, Clare!"

I step over to where she's standing, and I see my pie in its blue plate, the upper crust topped with another crust which I carved out to look like a big maple leaf. There's a blue ribbon beside it, along with a huge purple ribbon with gold letters: "Best of Show."

"Oh, my," I say. I've won a blue ribbon many times, but never best of show. I'll get an extra $15 plus the $15 for the first place in pies. I wonder who the judge is this year. Whoever it is, she's just made herself a fast friend.

I'm feeling right proud as we walk along, looking at the vegetable exhibits. "I can't believe there are so many!" Mrs. Langhorne says.

"You'll have to start your garden and exhibit next year," I say. She smiles her little half smile and says, "We'll see."

My squash and tomatoes arranged inside a whittled-down gourd wins second place for vegetable display, but there's no ribbon beside my cauliflower. Hattie Rogers' first-place cauliflower is quite a bit bigger, but I'll bet anything it's not as tender. Riley had suggested I enter my onions, which were really big this year, but I felt there was something special about that cauliflower. I look at it again and think that it wasn't the cauliflower's fault it didn't win. I displayed it on my green Fiesta dinnerplate. Maybe it would have looked better on a thinner yellow plate—like Hattie Rogers used. I push Hattie's plate back a little and move my plate forward, so they sit side by side, then give my cauliflower a little pat and move to the next table.

Riley's won a blue ribbon for his amber syrup. No surprise there. Riley's won a blue for syrup fifteen years running.

I dawdle over the flower arrangements and try to explain to Mrs. Langhorne the difference between an aster and an astilbe. She seems to want to learn, but when we're halfway down the table, she's disappeared. Finally, I spot her. She's at the end of the room, looking up at the photographs and paintings hung on pegboards attached to eight-foot-tall moveable stands.

As I head her way, I stop to study the needlework. My cousin Catherine's cross-stitch has won a blue ribbon. It's a nice little hanging, a picture of our covered bridge. She even stitched the words to the sign you see crossing from New Hampshire: "Walk Your Horses or Pay Two Dollars Fine."

When I reach Mrs. Langhorne, she's looking at a painting with a red ribbon pinned next to it. I realize it's her name at the bottom. Some things about that picture remind me of the famous French artist's painting she has hanging above her fireplace. I like this picture better. The river is wider, and it sparkles between stands of trees—big New Hampshire pine trees, a couple of sugar maples and, up close on the right, the leaning trunk of a paper birch. Mount Ascutney peeks out from between the pines.

"Look at that!" I say. "You didn't tell me you put a picture in the fair. And you won a ribbon!" People like to buy pictures that win ribbons, but Mrs. Langhorne has her picture tagged *Not For Sale.*

I'm thinking she should look happy, but there's a puzzled look to her face as she studies the blue-ribbon picture next to hers. At first, it just looks like a jumble of colors. Then, finally, I make out a fawn lying down in some grass. Beside the fawn, there's a pond with little yellow lilies floating, not in it, but across the sky above it. A big black signature slants across the bottom right corner. Most pictures displayed in the fair are listed for around $25. The tag next to this picture says $5,000!

"I know that painting," Mrs. Langhorne says, "but I don't recognize the name."

I peer at the signature. "Looks like Spencer Drake," I say. "He's the fellow who bought that mansion two driveways up the road from you."

Since he's rich enough to buy that big house, and he's put a $5,000 sticker on this picture, I'm believing that Mr. Spencer Drake must be a famous painter.

Mrs. Langhorne shakes her head. "Clare, listen. He didn't paint that picture. It was created nearly forty years ago by a New York artist named Hilda Halkinovitch. I know because, when I worked in a gallery back then, I sold that same painting to a young couple from Connecticut."

I'm thinking she can't be right, but I don't know how to tell her.

As we wander down the hill toward the midway, she tells me that the artist was a young woman with bright red hair, freckles and slate blue eyes. "She was the first artist we showed from a group that worked way downtown in wretched buildings on Coenties Street. She was living there in a one-room loft and would get up at five every morning to work eight hours at a bakery, then she would paint when she got off around three in the afternoon. That picture was an abstract from a photograph her father had taken when he was in the army in Germany."

Now I don't know what to think. Mr. Drake's painting might be similar to the one Mrs. Langhorne sold, but it can't be the same one since it's obvious that it's his name on the canvas.

Mrs. Langhorne tells me more. "This painting stuck in my mind because it was Hilda's first sale. I felt kind of bad, handing her the check for $350, which excluded the gallery charge of $150, but she was thrilled. Three hundred and fifty dollars seemed like a fortune to her—and she said that selling that painting validated all her hard work to become an artist. And now that thief is asking $5,000 for that same picture."

We leave the school and, as we approach the midway, I ask Mrs. Langhorne if we can stop a minute at the candied apple booth because I've been hankering for a sweet since I finished my hotdog at lunch. While we're waiting in line, I ask her if she sold any more of Hilda's paintings. She says the gallery owner upped the price to $600 on two more of Hilda's paintings. Both sold in a few weeks. Then Hilda moved her work to a pricier gallery uptown."

"Is she famous?" I ask.

"I wouldn't say she's famous, but her work is appreciated. Also, it's appreciated in price. As Spencer Drake must know. I bought one of her early paintings, a lovely abstract that made you feel like you were strolling through a tranquil forest glen. My late husband said it depressed him, so I gave it to a good friend—a professor. He hung it in his study and said that just looking at it made him feel content.

I'm taken aback for sure. I've received fake jewelry and bunches of flowers and such from friends, but the only picture I ever got wasn't even a painting. It was a copy of a picture by Maxfield Parrish that Riley thought would look good at the end of our hall. I wonder why Mrs. Langhorne would give this professor such an expensive gift, but I figure it's none of my business. She's a come-lately customer of Riley's business, not my long-time bosom friend.

When we get to the window of the Candy Apple stand, I order a bright red cinnamon apple. Mrs. Langhorne orders one, too, and slides five dollars over the counter—paying for us both. Maybe we're better friends than I thought.

◆◆◆

We're still munching on our apples when we get close to Riley's booth. The lady with the cane is putting a bunch of bills into the black pot, and another fellow is standing next to the scale. His name, Spencer, is on the chalkboard. I've only seen him a couple of times from a distance, but I know he's the same man who signed that blue-ribbon picture.

"It's him!" I whisper to Mrs. Langhorne. "That's Mr. Spencer Drake!"

We move forward. "There's a Centurian Club logo on his golf shirt," Mrs. Langhorne says. "That's a posh British club. Where is he from?"

"I'm not sure," I say. "Riley was up at his house repairing some cabinets and said he didn't know what to make of the fellow because most of the time he spoke like the King of England—but then he'd get rattled over something and sound like a moonshiner from Mississippi."

Riley writes something on the chalkboard and turns it around so folks in front of the booth can see.

SPENCER
AGE: 52
WEIGHT:178

Some folks nod.

Riley hands Mr. Drake the microphone and asks him to say his age.

"Fa-de-faur," he says.

"Forty-four?" Riley asks.

Spencer Drake raises an eyebrow. "Right. That's what I just said."

"How much do you weigh, sir?

"One-fifty-faur," he says.

Now I notice the handsome new deputy sheriff, Chad Cheever, standing next to me. He's not dressed in a uniform, but in jeans and a blue denim shirt. He doesn't move a muscle or ask me what's going on, but his dark eyes rove back and forth between the platform and the crowd like he's on duty.

Riley turns to the audience and points to the chalkboard. "He says he weighs one hundred and fifty-four. What do you think?"

The people in the crowd shake their heads and murmur, "no." A man with a long red beard removes his sunglasses and squints at the board. He's Simon LeClare, a foreman down at the Claremont mill.

"We're betting on you, Riley," he shouts out. "One hundred and seventy-eight."

The other folks nod.

Riley asks Spencer Drake to step up on the scale. Mr. Drake puts his right foot on the scale and leans forward. The arrow rises to 140 pounds.

"Looks like I lost some weight," he says.

"Both feet," Riley says.

Spencer Drake doesn't move.

"Okay, folks," Riley says. "I still say 178. If I'm wrong, I'll treat each of you who raise your hand to a cotton candy. Hold up your hand, all of you who think I'm wrong."

Folks around here, they know Riley. Nobody holds up a hand.

Simon LeClare puts his sunglasses back on and hollers: "Make him get all the way on the scale."

The folks in the crowd shuffle about and nod. Some shake their raised fists. Riley holds out his hand, as if to help Spencer Drake climb on the scale, but Mr. Drake steps back, taking his right foot off the scale.

Simon LeClare shouts again: "Hey, Mister, you have to prove Riley is wrong. Hand over your license!"

Spencer Drake looks down on LeClare and grins, like he doesn't believe what he's hearing.

"Okay," Riley says. "It looks like the folks want to see proof that I'm wrong. Please pull out your driver's license."

Spencer Drake laughs and leans into the microphone. "Royalty, old chap. I'm a close cousin to Princess Diana Spencer, you know. No license required. And, in case you're interested in my surname, I'm also a direct descendant of Sir Francis Drake."

◆◆◆

I've heard of Sir Francis—sailed all over the world, but I don't have any idea what he looked like. Princess Diana's face is on the TV all the time, and this man doesn't look anything like her. His skin is vanilla, not peaches and cream like Diana's. His eyes are small and gray and his nose skinny, leaning left like it's been busted.

Just then Mrs. Langhorne says to me: "He's lying."

Deputy Chad Cheever steps closer to us as Mrs. Langhorne adds, "The queen is the only royalty that doesn't need to have a driving license. And Sir

Francis Drake was married twice but left no direct heirs."

I'm shaking my head, wondering how she could know that stuff.

"My father always told me we were descended from Sir Francis," she says, "but since Drake never had any children, that's impossible. My great, great grandfather married a Drake, but she wasn't Sir Francis' daughter. A sister? A cousin? I never could figure it out. All I know for sure—and I'm glad of it—none of my ancestors inherited any of Sir Francis' plundered loot. Also, we never claimed someone else's painting as our own."

Deputy Cheever nods to us and saunters up to the right edge of the platform. Riley greets him with a little salute, then picks up the mike. I can tell he wants to get rid of this so-called Spencer Drake fellow and bring the next customer up to the scale.

"Well, shucks," Riley says. "I guess I missed on both age and weight. That's a first for the '94 fair. Here's two free cotton candy tickets for you, Sir Spencer Drake."

Mr. Drake sticks out his hand, but Riley's still holding onto the tickets. "Maybe you'd like to share one with our new police officer, here," he says and smiles down at Deputy Cheever. The folks chuckle.

Mr. Drake doesn't take the tickets. Instead, he jumps down from the left side of the platform and slithers away toward the parking lot. Riley turns to hand the tickets to Chad Cheever, but the deputy has already disappeared into the crowd. He seems to be chasing after Mr. Drake.

Scuttlebutt says that when Deputy Cheever and the Sheriff showed up at Spencer Drake's house Saturday night, he was gone. The maid said Mr. Drake left her a hundred-dollar bill to tide her over for a while but didn't say when he'd be back. His sporty little green Aston Martin was not in the garage, and his blue-ribbon painting—and the blue ribbon itself—were missing from the fair.

◆◆◆

Sunday evening, I go down to Town Hall to pick up my winnings. Mrs. Langhorne is walking out the door with her painting, a prize money envelope and—what do you know—a blue ribbon. I guess they upped her award when that Drake fellow made off with his picture.

"Why look at you," I say. "First time you entered, too. Your picture will be in the *Upper Valley News*, and the Windsor Craft Store will be after you to exhibit some paintings to sell."

"There's some fine work in that store," Mrs. Langhorne says. "Especially Gary Milek and Sabra Field. If I ever produce a painting as good as the least of theirs, I might consider offering some to sell."

She holds her painting out at arm's length and looks it over. "I didn't enter the fair expecting to win a ribbon," she says. "I just knew I had to work up the courage to exhibit my work for other people to see. Then maybe I'd know how it feels to be a real artist."

I'm thinking she must be joshing me. Who would go to the trouble of entering unless they wanted to win a prize?

But she looks serious and keeps on talking. "Clare, you know that winning doesn't make you better than someone else. It just means one person— the judge—likes your entry. Or maybe the judge doesn't like what anyone submitted, but she has to give someone a ribbon. So, she goes 'eeny-meeny-miney-mo' and the 'mo' lands on your entry."

"Well," I say, "maybe that goes for paintings and such, but pies don't all taste the same."

"Oh, Clare," she says, "what if you were judging the pies and you never liked banana creme pie or huckleberry pie. Would those pies have a chance of winning?"

"I like every kind of pie," I say. "And, besides, a judge should like every kind of art or quilt or pie or vegetable or whatever it is they're judging— otherwise it's not proper."

Mrs. Langhorne smiles her little smile, but I'm not ready to give in.

"Judges shouldn't be so quick to judge," I say. "If a judge doesn't know what they're doing, they might give a prize to the biggest cauliflower in the show, or one that's on a pretty plate. But a smaller cauliflower might taste better. I like them smaller."

"Me, too," Mrs. Langhorne says. Now she gives me a wicked big grin and heads off to her car.

I go inside to pick up my entries—Riley's blue-ribbon syrup; my best in show Hubbard squash pie; my red ribbon squash and tomatoes and my cauliflower that didn't win a thing.

I heft the cauliflower in my hand. It still smells fresh. It feels tender. Maybe it is a little small, but, like Mrs. Langhorne said, at least I had the courage to enter it.

WHAT MAKES SONIA CONTENT

Autumn

My first summer in New England glides into September. Then, mid-month, the nights take on a decided chill and, a few weeks later, the hillsides turn to a dazzling blend of orange, red and gold. Every third car on the highway has an out-of-state license plate: New York, New Jersey, Ohio, Massachusetts, Virginia, Michigan.

I marvel at the vibrant maples, oaks, sycamores and hawthorns, and the landscape painting I started yesterday seems brighter, more intense than the one I finished two days ago.

But as daylight decreases, photosynthesis and chlorophyll wane, and leaf veins begin to shutter down. Even the lightest wind sends the first leaves spinning from their stems.

Day by day, the ground becomes colder, and graying leaves settle like quilts beneath the skeletal trees. My new painting is more somber than the last.

Still, I slowly begin to realize that even the oncoming dormant season offers possibilities. Endless possibilities.

I wash out my brushes, lay aside my paints and accept with pleasure a dinner party invitation. My now-retired neighbors trade stories about living in Tel Aviv, Dar es Salaam and Tehran.

"We spent four days in an underground bomb shelter."

"The stores were empty. No milk, no meat to be found."

"And then the dog slipped into an open sewer."

"But, still, we were happy there."

"Our children learned to realize how privileged they were."

"Our children developed empathy at such an early age."

"We were content."

Someday I may want to travel again. Petra, perhaps? Cape Town? Kyoto? For now, I am content to be welcomed as a guest at my neighbor's dinner table.

Across the Covered Bridge

◆◆◆

The sun rises to reveal the first overnight frost. The driveway is slick with a mix of rain and snow, and the grass, the plants, the fallen leaves are gilded silvery white. By afternoon, the weeds in my overgrown garden have wilted and turned a slimy yellow.

I track down Sakura Ishii, the Japanese exchange student I met at the Dartmouth bookstore. She comes for tea and begins to teach me haiku. Tonight, I play with a new painting with the hope that a poem will emerge.

hunter's moon
hanging from the highest branch
one last maple leaf

Will I ever master this ancient art? For now, I'm content with knowing I still have much to learn.

Winter

The snow coats the needles of the white pine, black spruce and hemlock trees. The wind rises, and clumps of snow drop from the needles. A black-capped chickadee lands on my kitchen windowsill. She fluffs up her feathers and pecks at the seeds in the feeder. She whistles *fee-bee-bee*. A branch snaps. It lingers, hanging from the tree, then finally drops to the ground. Thump. A higher branch falls. A louder thump. The chickadee tosses her head and flies out of sight.

Riley, my handyman, pulls into my driveway to change the broken lock on my front door. While he's working, I ask him about the history of this town. "Back in 1763," he says, "this place was a port for tall masts cut from the white pine that grew all around here. The masts were floated down the river then shipped to England. I've been told that the Royal Navy had some 250 sloops, schooners and frigates—but no big trees to turn into masts. Did you know that, when the town was incorporated, it was named for a British vice admiral?"

I had no idea. "Tell me more," I say.

Riley tests the lock, hands me the key and continues. "When I was in the Navy, I learned that during the Revolutionary War, the British Navy sent hundreds of ships over here—and I bet that many of them were masted with our pine trees. The colonies only had twenty-seven Naval ships to protect our shores and battle the Royal Navy fleet. But Privateers went after the English merchant ships."

Riley grins. "It was them and John Paul Jones that helped us lick the Limeys."

Riley packs up his tools, opens the door and looks through the bare trees toward the river. "That bridge was built in 1866—the longest two-span covered bridge in the world. An ice-out in 1977 tore it up good, and it got in such bad shape that it was closed to traffic in '87." He shakes his head, then smiles. "Believe me, there was quite a party down at the bridge when it reopened in December of '89. The whole town turned out for the celebration. There were bands and big shots from both New Hampshire and Vermont. Even both governors were there.

Tonight, I settle down on my couch with Jerome Wikoff's book on the Connecticut River. If I read enough of the history of this place, will I discover how to belong?

For now, I'm content to read.

♦♦♦

Snow coats my roof, my steps and windowsills and hides the pile of blackened, soggy needles beneath the big white pine outside my front window. The plow arrives, scrapes the asphalt and leaves ridges of snow along each side of the driveway.

The congenial, gray-haired snowplow driver stops his truck by the front door and looks expectantly toward the house. He has deep-set eyes and a handsomely sculptured face and physique. What if I invite him in for a cup of coffee?

Or what if I call that late 40-ish man with a chevron mustache and ask him to stop by for a drink tonight? I understand he has a penchant for marrying older women—and is currently between wives.

When I consider how these scenarios might play out, I realize that I haven't had enough time to refill my heart with the amount of love a partner deserves. Though I tossed away the trappings of my married life, I haven't ceased mourning the man who—for better or for worse—was my husband for just shy of forty years. For now, I'm content with memory.

◆◆◆

The snow is waist-high, the sun is shining, and the thermometer by my back door reads a balmy 30 degrees. Though the plow went through early this morning, the roads are already dry. Still, as I pass the cemetery at the bottom of my hill, I notice two-foot-high cones of snow resting peacefully atop each of the old monuments.

I turn onto the highway, then take the next left to park at the turnaround leading to the unplowed river road. The center of the road has become a smooth trail, packed down by our neighbors' snowshoes and skis. My new friend, Phyllis, a writer, is waiting beside her car. She's wearing a sleek white snow suit with a fur-lined hood and matching white ski gloves. As always, she looks stunning.

We unload our gear, knock the snow from our boots, step into our skis and lock them in place. Before I even settle into my stance, Phyllis is a hundred yards ahead of me.

Today, my third day of skiing with Phyllis, I feel more comfortable moving on these long, flat sticks attached to my feet. I'm gliding more than shuffling, and my poles are moving almost in rhythm with my feet. But I still can't keep pace with Phyllis. She's some three hundred yards ahead when she stops, step-turns her skis to face me and gives me a thumbs up. When I catch up with her, she smiles and says, "You're looking good."

I'm wearing my old brown puffy jacket, my son's faded green woolen gloves and toque, and I know I need to do some serious clothes shopping if I'm ever to look anywhere near as good as Phyllis. But I do feel as if I'm beginning to get the hang of skiing. I take off ahead of her and pick up my pace, though, again, she glides right past me.

The next time I catch up with Phyllis, she's stopped at a bend that overlooks the river, now a glistening field filled with balls of ice. Here and there, small rivulets of water emerge from the ice and wend their way south toward the bridge. Otherwise, except for the occasional burble or crack, the river is still.

In the spring, I will follow this road to its end, then climb up the hill to sit beneath the sheltering oak on Maxfield Parrish's lawn. I'll try to imagine our lush valley as Parrish imagined it. But, for now, I'm content to stand in silence beside a friend, both of us gazing down on a river that appears to have ceased to flow.

♦♦♦

I've been stoking my wood stove for months now, and this morning three-foot-long icicles descend from the eaves over the back door. The outside thermometer hovers at ten below zero.

I bundle up in my old wool sweater, my now-ragged down jacket and calf-length snow boots and walk down the driveway to retrieve the newspaper from the box. My right foot slips on a patch of ice three feet from the box, but I manage to stay upright long enough to grab onto the post. I stuff the paper under my arm and climb more carefully back up the hill.

There's not much news is today's paper, but I pour another cup of coffee and reread a notice on page five. A puppy, a Black Labrador mix with inquisitive eyes and floppy ears, is free to a good home.

I want that puppy. I have a good home.

I imagine coming home to a puppy wagging his tail. I'd place a bowl of food down on the mudroom floor, and he'd look up at me in appreciation. He'd sleep at my feet while I paint and snuggle up against me on the living room couch while I read. I'd name him Pal.

In the summer, I'd take him up the hill to the creek. He'd swim in the beaver pond. I'd wash him off with the garden hose and rub him down with a warm towel. I'd buy him a dozen rubbery balls. Riley would build him a big fence.

But would I want to walk Pal when it's ten below and there are patches of ice on the driveway? When he's twelve years old, he'd be nearly my age in dog years. Would I be able to care for him? Would I have the strength, if needed, to lift him into the car? Would I still be alive?

Riley's told me that he's looking for a good dog. I call to tell him about the notice in the paper. His wife, Clare, answers the phone and says that Riley is already on his way to check out that same dog. I tell her the dog's name is Pal, and I hope that Riley will bring him to stay with me from time to time. That might make me content enough.

Spring

Yesterday it was twenty-four degrees; today it's fifty and sunny. Next week it's predicted to be in the mid-forties, often with bouts of rain.

Riley brings Pal to visit. Sometimes, when both he and his wife are working, he'll leave Pal with me for an entire afternoon. Susannah, a neighbor's girl, who proudly tells me that she's almost eight, runs from her house, pigtails flying, when she sees me walking Pal up the road. Today we take a rest on the little bridge below the beaver dam, and Susannah pets Pal profusely. She tells him about the bears and monkeys and donkeys who live vividly in books she's read.

Both Pal and I are content to listen.

♦♦♦

The river roars with churning ice which breaks into enormous shards and rushes toward the covered bridge, sometimes slamming into the piles. From Phyllis's yard, high up on a bank, I watch the ice toss up a whole tree, a neighbor's back deck, a tire, a hog, a child's twisted pink bicycle.

The following days bring sun, rain, snowmelt, mud. The fields, gardens, ditches, the unpaved roads, even the hallowed cemetery grounds have turned to mud. But here and there—at the turn of the river, on the lower branches of Maxfield Parrish's big oak, in the bushes near town hall—I begin to notice touches of silvery green.

♦♦♦

Since I arrived here last May, I've been working at my easel and have some half a dozen impressionist landscapes that might be good enough to sell. I've taken them over to the state craft store and gallery across the river and, today, a week later, I receive a call. I've been juried in. I've been accepted by a panel of artists.

I'm a painter. An artist. That's me.

Until today, I was just an eccentric old woman pretending to be an artist. I was a stranger who impulsively squandered a grand lifestyle to move to a shabby cottage with a single treasure—a work of art which may or may not be worth a fortune. Until today, I might have called myself a widow, a mother, a person who once studied art, a woman who spent a great deal of money supporting promising painters.

Finally, today, I believe I've stumbled into becoming who I was meant to be. I'm an artist, and, even better, I'm a never-to-be-famous artist. Nobody will purchase my work because they believe it will increase in value.

But a few of my small paintings might hang on a home or office wall. An owner of one of my pictures might stop from time to time to reflect on my river, my mountain, my sugar maple, my covered bridge. They may see something in that painting that I never saw and, if so, I am content.

Sally Stiles

WITH GRADITUDE:

To writers John Conlee, Kathleen Toomey Jabs, James Tobin and Len Shartzer who never cease to inspire me.

To Louise and Roger Crowley for detouring from their route to take pictures of the bridge—and again to Louise for her continued encouragement.

To artists Augustus Saint-Gaudens and Maxfield Parrish whose creative energy continues to flow through the upper Connecticut River valley.

To contemporary artists whom I admire for their captivating work, especially Sarah and Gary Milek, Sabra Field, Vonnie Whitworth, Laura Edwards, Diane Ainsworth, Kay Gerehart, Andy Smith, Faye Judson, Richard Toft, Patricia Lassiter, Thomas Quaye and Bruce Onobrakpeya.

To Bonnie Levine whose love of Cezanne permeates these stories.

To Beverly Peterson and Cory Ragsdale whose reviews of the manuscript were invaluable.

To Joe and Amanda Wareing for listening so well.

To Carol-Lynn Marrazzo for her generous insider help on so-important details.

To Phyllis Barber who, once again, urged me on to completion.

To Bret Lott, who believed in Will's vision.

Also, to Katheryn Lovell, who graciously refused to find errors in the manuscript.

To talented New England writers W.D. Wetherell, Sydney Lea, Norman Maclean, Howard Frank Mosher, Dalia Pagani, Louise Erdrich and Melissa Mather for the vivid landscapes and lives they created.

To Virginia Colby and Hugh Wade for recording the history of an exceptional town.

To Alma Gilbert and John Dryfhout for chronicling the works of Maxfield Parrish and Augustus Saint-Gaudens.

To the late Rose LaClair of Cornish who often beseeched the Virgin to send me inspiration.

To former Vermont and New Hampshire residents Eric and Margaret Rothchild, Anthony and Ann Neidecker, Joseph and Prue Dennis, John and Connie White, Jim and Dusty Hardy for your welcoming friendship—and for hosting dinner parties well worth attending.

To dependable handymen and snowplow drivers everywhere.

And, of course, to David, who found us a special home upriver from a covered bridge.

Sally Stiles

ACCLAIM FOR
ACROSS THE COVERED BRIDGE

"Sally Stiles' collection of linked tales, *Across the Covered Bridge,* superbly fulfills a brilliant artistic concept. Individually, her snapshots from a life are charming and engaging; collectively, they amount to much more."—Professor John Conlee, author of nine novels, including *The Rarest Book in the World.*

"A Cezanne painting and a poem scribbled on a boy's baseball glove help to transform a woman into the person she was always meant to be. Sally Stiles' beautiful and insightful writing brings to life a fascinating character you will love and always remember."
– J.E. Tobin, author of *When We Were Wolves* and *The Triple Divide.*

"I loved it! These nine stories offer a bridge to self-discovery; an arch over a flow of vibrant imagery."
—Greg Lilly, author of *Stray* and nine other books.

In *Across the Covered Bridge*, Sally Stiles unveils a tucked-away world filled with remarkable creativity, rich characters, and deep compassion for our all-too-human journeys.—Kathleen T. Jabs, author of *Black Wings*

"This book inspires me." –Prof. Beverly Peterson

Printed in the USA
CPSIA information can be obtained
at www.ICGtesting.com
JSHW020340300124
56285JS00001B/55